BASEBALL IN APRIL

BASEBALL
IN APRIL
AND
OTHER
STORIES

GARY SOTO

HARCOURT BRACE & COMPANY

San Diego   New York   London

Requests for permission to make copies of any
part of the work should be mailed to:
Permissions Department,
Harcourt Brace & Company,
6277 Sea Harbor Drive,
Orlando, Florida 32887-6777.

"La Bamba" (Ritchie Valens) © 1958 Picture Our Music.
Administered by Warner-Tamerlane Publishing Corp.
All rights reserved. Used by permission.

"La Bamba" first appeared in *Fiction Network*,
Spring/Summer, 1989, and a version of
"Baseball in April" appeared in
Living up the Street (Strawberry Hill Press, 1985).

Library of Congress Cataloging-in-Publication Data
Soto, Gary.
    Baseball in April and other stories/by Gary Soto—1st ed.
        p.   cm.
Summary: A collection of eleven short stories focusing
on the everyday adventures of Hispanic young people
growing up in Fresno, California.
    ISBN 0-15-205720-X
    1. Children's stories, American. [1. Mexican Americans—
California—Fiction. 2. Short stories.]   I. Title.
PZ7.S7242Bas   1990
[Fic]—dc20   89-36460

Designed by Trina Stahl
Printed in the United States of America

J I H G F E

For all the "karate kids" in the country and for Julius Baker, Jr., teacher of some of these kids.

CONTENTS

BASEBALL IN APRIL

BROKEN CHAIN

Alfonso sat on the porch trying to push his crooked teeth to where he thought they belonged. He hated the way he looked. Last week he did fifty sit-ups a day, thinking that he would burn those already apparent ripples on his stomach to even deeper ripples, dark ones, so when he went swimming at the canal next summer, girls in cut-offs would notice. And the guys would think he was tough, someone who could take a punch and give it back. He wanted "cuts" like those he had seen on a calendar of an Aztec warrior standing on a pyramid with a woman in his arms. (Even she had cuts he could see beneath her thin dress.) The calendar hung above the cash register at La Plaza. Orsua, the owner, said Alfonso could have the calendar at the end of the year if the waitress, Yolanda, didn't take it first.

Alfonso studied the magazine pictures of rock stars for a hairstyle. He liked the way Prince looked—and the bass player from Los Lobos. Alfonso thought he would look cool with his hair razored into a V in the back and streaked purple. But he knew his mother wouldn't go for it. And his father, who was *puro Mexicano,* would sit in his chair after work, sullen as a toad, and call him "sissy."

Alfonso didn't dare color his hair. But one day he had had it butched on the top, like in the magazines. His father had come home that evening from a softball game, happy that his team had drilled four homers in a thirteen-to-five bashing of Color Tile. He'd swaggered into the living room, but had stopped cold when he saw Alfonso and asked, not joking but with real concern, "Did you hurt your head at school? *Qué pasó?*"

Alfonso had pretended not to hear his father and had gone to his room, where he studied his hair from all angles in the mirror. He liked what he saw until he smiled and realized for the first time that his teeth were crooked, like a pile of wrecked cars. He grew depressed and turned away from the mirror. He sat on his bed and leafed through the rock magazine until he came to the rock star with the butched top. His mouth was closed, but Alfonso was sure his teeth weren't crooked.

Alfonso didn't want to be the handsomest kid at school, but he was determined to be better-looking than average. The next day he spent his lawn-mowing money on a new shirt, and, with a pocketknife, scooped the moons of dirt from under his fingernails.

He spent hours in front of the mirror trying to herd his teeth into place with his thumb. He asked his mother if he could have braces, like Frankie Molina, her godson, but he asked at the wrong time. She was at the kitchen table licking the envelope to the house payment. She glared up at him. "Do you think money grows on trees?"

His mother clipped coupons from magazines and newspapers, kept a vegetable garden in the summer, and shopped at Penney's and K-Mart. Their family ate a lot of *frijoles,* which was OK because nothing else tasted so good, though one time Alfonso had had Chinese pot stickers and thought they were the next best food in the world.

He didn't ask his mother for braces again, even when she was in a better mood. He decided to fix his teeth by pushing on them with his thumbs. After breakfast that Saturday he went to his room, closed the door quietly, turned the radio on, and pushed for three hours straight.

He pushed for ten minutes, rested for five, and every half hour, during a radio commercial, checked to see if his smile had improved. It hadn't.

Eventually he grew bored and went outside with an old gym sock to wipe down his bike, a ten-speed from Montgomery Ward. His thumbs were tired and wrinkled and pink, the way they got when he stayed in the bathtub too long.

Alfonso's older brother, Ernie, rode up on *his* Montgomery Ward bicycle looking depressed. He parked his bike against the peach tree and sat on the back steps, keeping his head down and stepping on ants that came too close.

Alfonso knew better than to say anything when Ernie looked mad. He turned his bike over, balancing it on the handlebars and seat, and flossed the spokes with the sock. When he was finished, he pressed a knuckle to his teeth until they tingled.

Ernie groaned and said, "Ah, man."

Alfonso waited a few minutes before asking, "What's the matter?" He pretended not to be too interested. He picked up a wad of steel wool and continued cleaning the spokes.

Ernie hesitated, not sure if Alfonso would laugh. But it came out. "Those girls didn't show up. And you better not laugh."

"What girls?"

Then Alfonso remembered his brother bragging about how he and Frostie met two girls from Kings Canyon Junior High last week on Halloween night. They were dressed as gypsies, the costume for all poor Chicanas—they just had to borrow scarves and gaudy red lipstick from their *abuelitas.*

Alfonso walked over to his brother. He compared their two bikes: his gleamed like a handful of dimes, while Ernie's looked dirty.

"They said we were supposed to wait at the corner. But they didn't show up. Me and Frostie waited and waited like *pendejos.* They were playing games with us."

Alfonso thought that was a pretty dirty trick but sort of funny too. He would have to try that some day.

"Were they cute?" Alfonso asked.

"I guess so."

"Do you think you could recognize them?"

"If they were wearing red lipstick, maybe."

Alfonso sat with his brother in silence, both of them smearing ants with their floppy high tops. Girls could sure act weird, especially the ones you meet on Halloween.

Later that day, Alfonso sat on the porch pressing on his teeth. Press, relax; press, relax. His portable radio was on, but not loud enough to make Mr. Rojas come down the steps and wave his cane at him.

Alfonso's father drove up. Alfonso could tell by the way he sat in his truck, a Datsun with a different-colored front fender, that his team had lost their softball game. Alfonso got off the porch in a hurry because he knew his father would be in a bad mood. He went to the backyard, where he unlocked his bike, sat on it with the kickstand down, and pressed on his teeth. He punched himself in the stomach, and growled, "Cuts." Then he patted his butch and whispered, "Fresh."

After a while Alfonso pedaled up the street, hands in his pockets, toward Foster's Freeze, where he was chased by a ratlike Chihuahua. At his old school, John Burroughs Elementary, he found a kid hanging upside down on the top of a barbed-wire fence with a girl looking up at him. Alfonso skidded to a stop and helped the kid untangle his pants from the barbed wire. The kid was grateful. He had been afraid he would have to stay up there all night. His sister, who was Alfonso's age, was also grateful. If she had to go home and tell her mother that Frankie was stuck on a fence and couldn't get down, she would get scolded.

"Thanks," she said. "What's your name?"

Alfonso remembered her from his school and noticed that she was kind of cute, with ponytails and straight teeth. "Alfonso. You go to my school, huh?"

"Yeah. I've seen you around. You live nearby?"

"Over on Madison."

"My uncle used to live on that street, but he moved to Stockton."

"Stockton's near Sacramento, isn't it?"

"You been there?"

"No." Alfonso looked down at his shoes. He wanted to say something clever the way people do on TV. But the

5

only thing he could think to say was that the governor lived in Sacramento. As soon as he shared this observation, he winced inside.

Alfonso walked with the girl and the boy as they started for home. They didn't talk much. Every few steps, the girl, whose name was Sandra, would look at him out of the corner of her eye, and Alfonso would look away. He learned that she was in seventh grade, just like him, and that she had a pet terrier named Queenie. Her father was a mechanic at Rudy's Speedy Repair, and her mother was a teacher's aide at Jefferson Elementary.

When they came to the street, Alfonso and Sandra stopped at her corner, but her brother ran home. Alfonso watched him stop in the front yard to talk to a lady he guessed was their mother. She was raking leaves into a pile.

"I live over there," she said, pointing.

Alfonso looked over her shoulder for a long time, trying to muster enough nerve to ask her if she'd like to go bike riding tomorrow.

Shyly, he asked, "You wanna go bike riding?"

"Maybe." She played with a ponytail and crossed one leg in front of the other. "But my bike has a flat."

"I can get my brother's bike. He won't mind."

She thought a moment before she said, "OK. But not tomorrow. I have to go to my aunt's."

"How about after school on Monday?"

"I have to take care of my brother until my mom comes home from work. How 'bout four-thirty?"

"OK," he said. "Four-thirty." Instead of parting immediately, they talked for a while, asking questions like,

"Who's your favorite group?" "Have you ever been on the Big Dipper at Santa Cruz?" and "Have you ever tasted pot stickers?" But the question-and-answer period ended when Sandra's mother called her home.

Alfonso took off as fast he could on his bike, jumped the curb, and, cool as he could be, raced away with his hands stuffed in his pockets. But when he looked back over his shoulder, the wind raking through his butch, Sandra wasn't even looking. She was already on her lawn, heading for the porch.

That night he took a bath, pampered his hair into place, and did more than his usual set of exercises. In bed, in between the push-and-rest on his teeth, he pestered his brother to let him borrow his bike.

"Come on, Ernie," he whined. "Just for an hour."

"*Chale,* I might want to use it."

"Come on, man, I'll let you have my trick-or-treat candy."

"What you got?"

"Three baby Milky Ways and some Skittles."

"Who's going to use it?"

Alfonso hesitated, then risked the truth. "I met this girl. She doesn't live too far."

Ernie rolled over on his stomach and stared at the outline of his brother, whose head was resting on his elbow. "*You* got a girlfriend?"

"She ain't my girlfriend, just a girl."

"What does she look like?"

"Like a girl."

"Come on, what does she look like?"

"She's got ponytails and a little brother."

"Ponytails! Those girls who messed with Frostie and me had ponytails. Is she cool?"

"I think so."

Ernie sat up in bed. "I bet you that's her."

Alfonso felt his stomach knot up. "She's going to be my girlfriend, not yours!"

"I'm going to get even with her!"

"You better not touch her," Alfonso snarled, throwing a wadded Kleenex at him. "I'll run you over with my bike."

For the next hour, until their mother threatened them from the living room to be quiet or else, they argued whether it was the same girl who had stood Ernie up. Alfonso said over and over that she was too nice to pull a stunt like that. But Ernie argued that she lived only two blocks from where those girls had told them to wait, that she was in the same grade, and, the clincher, that she had ponytails. Secretly, however, Ernie was jealous that his brother, two years younger than himself, might have found a girlfriend.

Sunday morning, Ernie and Alfonso stayed away from each other, though over breakfast they fought over the last tortilla. Their mother, sewing at the kitchen table, warned them to knock it off. At church they made faces at one another when the priest, Father Jerry, wasn't looking. Ernie punched Alfonso in the arm, and Alfonso, his eyes wide with anger, punched back.

Monday morning they hurried to school on their bikes, neither saying a word, though they rode side by side. In first period, Alfonso worried himself sick. How would he borrow a bike for her? He considered asking his best friend, Raul, for his bike. But Alfonso knew Raul, a paper boy with dollar signs in his eyes, would charge him, and he had less than sixty cents, counting the soda bottles he could cash.

Between history and math, Alfonso saw Sandra and her girlfriend huddling at their lockers. He hurried by without being seen.

During lunch Alfonso hid in metal shop so he wouldn't run into Sandra. What would he say to her? If he weren't mad at his brother, he could ask Ernie what girls and guys talk about. But he *was* mad, and anyway, Ernie was pitching nickels with his friends.

Alfonso hurried home after school. He did the morning dishes as his mother had asked and raked the leaves. After finishing his chores, he did a hundred sit-ups, pushed on his teeth until they hurt, showered, and combed his hair into a perfect butch. He then stepped out to the patio to clean his bike. On an impulse, he removed the chain to wipe off the gritty oil. But while he was unhooking it from the back sprocket, it snapped. The chain lay in his hand like a dead snake.

Alfonso couldn't believe his luck. Now, not only did he not have an extra bike for Sandra, he had no bike for himself. Frustrated, and on the verge of tears, he flung the chain as far as he could. It landed with a hard slap against the back fence and spooked his sleeping cat, Benny. Benny looked around, blinking his soft gray eyes, and went back to sleep.

Alfonso retrieved the chain, which was hopelessly broken. He cursed himself for being stupid, yelled at his bike for being cheap, and slammed the chain onto the cement. The chain snapped in another place and hit him when it popped up, slicing his hand like a snake's fang.

"Ow!" he cried, his mouth immediately going to his hand to suck on the wound.

After a dab of iodine, which only made his cut hurt

9

more, and a lot of thought, he went to the bedroom to plead with Ernie, who was changing to his after-school clothes.

"Come on, man, let me use it," Alfonso pleaded. "Please, Ernie, I'll do anything."

Although Ernie could see Alfonso's desperation, he had plans with his friend Raymundo. They were going to catch frogs at the Mayfair canal. He felt sorry for his brother, and gave him a stick of gum to make him feel better, but there was nothing he could do. The canal was three miles away, and the frogs were waiting.

Alfonso took the stick of gum, placed it in his shirt pocket, and left the bedroom with his head down. He went outside, slamming the screen door behind him, and sat in the alley behind his house. A sparrow landed in the weeds, and when it tried to come close, Alfonso screamed for it to scram. The sparrow responded with a squeaky chirp and flew away.

At four he decided to get it over with and started walking to Sandra's house, trudging slowly, as if he were waist-deep in water. Shame colored his face. How could he disappoint his first date? She would probably laugh. She might even call him *menso*.

He stopped at the corner where they were supposed to meet and watched her house. But there was no one outside, only a rake leaning against the steps.

Why did he have to take the chain off? he scolded himself. He always messed things up when he tried to take them apart, like the time he tried to repad his baseball mitt. He had unlaced the mitt and filled the pocket with cotton balls. But when he tried to put it back together, he had forgotten how it laced up. Everything became tangled like kite string. When he showed the mess to his mother, who was at the stove cooking dinner, she scolded him but put it back together and didn't tell his father what a dumb thing he had done.

Now he had to face Sandra and say, "I broke my bike, and my stingy brother took off on his."

He waited at the corner a few minutes, hiding behind a hedge for what seemed like forever. Just as he was starting to think about going home, he heard footsteps and knew it was too late. His hands, moist from worry, hung at his sides, and a thread of sweat raced down his armpit.

He peeked through the hedge. She was wearing a sweater with a checkerboard pattern. A red purse was slung over her shoulder. He could see her looking for him, standing on tiptoe to see if he was coming around the corner.

What have I done? Alfonso thought. He bit his lip, called himself *menso,* and pounded his palm against his forehead. Someone slapped the back of his head. He turned around and saw Ernie.

"We got the frogs, Alfonso," he said, holding up a wiggling plastic bag. "I'll show you later."

Ernie looked through the hedge, with one eye closed, at the girl. "She's not the one who messed with Frostie and me," he said finally. "You still wanna borrow my bike?"

Alfonso couldn't believe his luck. What a brother! What a pal! He promised to take Ernie's turn next time it was his turn to do the dishes. Ernie hopped on Raymundo's handlebars and said he would remember that promise. Then he was gone as they took off without looking back.

Free of worry now that his brother had come through, Alfonso emerged from behind the hedge with Ernie's bike, which was mud-splashed but better than nothing. Sandra waved.

"Hi," she said.

"Hi," he said back.

She looked cheerful. Alfonso told her his bike was broken and asked if she wanted to ride with him.

"Sounds good," she said, and jumped on the crossbar.

It took all of Alfonso's strength to steady the bike. He started off slowly, gritting his teeth, because she was heavier than he thought. But once he got going, it got easier. He pedaled smoothly, sometimes with only one hand on the handlebars, as they sped up one street and down another. Whenever he ran over a pothole, which was often, she screamed with delight, and once, when it looked like they were going to crash, she placed her hand over his, and it felt like love.

BASEBALL
IN APRIL

The night before Michael and Jesse were to try out for the Little League team for the third year in a row, the two brothers sat in their bedroom listening to the radio, pounding their fists into their gloves, and talking about how they would bend to pick up grounders or wave off another player and make the pop-up catch. "This is the year," Michael said with the confidence of an older brother. He pretended to scoop up the ball and throw out a man racing to first. He pounded his glove, looked at Jesse, and asked, "How'd you like that?"

When they reached Romain playground the next day there were a hundred kids divided into lines by age group: nine, ten, and eleven. Michael and Jesse stood in line, gloves hanging limp from their hands, and waited to have a large paper number pinned to their backs so that the field coaches would know who they were.

Jesse chewed his palm as he moved up the line. When his number was called he ran out onto the field to the sound of his black sneakers smacking against the clay. He looked at the kids still in line, then at Michael who yelled, "You can do it!" The first grounder, a three-bouncer, spun off his glove into center field. Another grounder cracked off the bat, and he scooped it up, but the ball rolled off his glove. Jesse stared at it before he picked it up and hurled it to first base. The next one he managed to pick up cleanly, but his throw made the first baseman leap into the air with an exaggerated grunt that made *him* look good. Three more balls were hit to Jesse, and he came up with one.

His number flapped like a broken wing as he ran off the field to sit in the bleachers and wait for Michael to trot onto the field.

Michael raced after the first grounder and threw it on the run. On the next grounder, he lowered himself to one knee and threw nonchalantly to first. As his number, a crooked seventeen, flapped on his back, he saw a coach make a mark on his clipboard.

Michael lunged at the next hit but missed, and it skidded into center field. He shaded his eyes after the next hit, a high pop-up, and when the ball came down he was there to slap it into his glove. His mouth grew fat from trying to hold back a smile. The coach made another mark on his clipboard.

When the next number was called, Michael jogged off the field with his head held high. He sat next to his brother, both dark and serious as they watched the other boys trot on and off the field.

Finally, the coaches told them to return after lunch for batting tryouts. Michael and Jesse ran home to eat a sandwich and talk about what to expect in the afternoon.

"Don't be scared," Michael said with his mouth full of ham sandwich, though he knew Jesse's batting was no good. He showed him how to stand. He spread his legs, worked his left foot into the carpet as if he were putting out a cigarette, and glared at where the ball would come from, twenty feet in front of him near the kitchen table. He swung an invisible bat, choked up on the handle, and swung again.

He turned to his younger brother. "Got it?"

Jesse said he thought he did and imitated Michael's swing until Michael said, "Yeah, you got it."

Jesse felt proud walking to the playground because the smaller kids were in awe of the paper number on his back. It was as if he were a soldier going off to war.

"Where you goin'?" asked Rosie, sister of Johnnie Serna, the playground bully. She had a large bag of sunflower seeds, and spat out a shell.

"Tryouts," Jesse said, barely looking at her as he kept stride with Michael.

At the diamond, Jesse once again grew nervous. He got into the line of nine-year-olds and waited for his turn at bat. Fathers clung to the fence, giving last-minute instructions to their kids.

By the time it was Jesse's turn, he was trembling and trying to catch Michael's eye for reassurance. He walked to the batter's box, tapped the bat on the plate—something he had seen many times on television—and waited. The first pitch was outside and over his head. The coach laughed.

He swung hard at the next pitch, spinning the ball foul. He tapped his bat again, kicked the dirt, and stepped into the batter's box. He swung at a low ball. Then he wound up and sliced the next ball foul to the edge of the infield grass, which surprised him because he didn't know he had the strength to send it that far.

Jesse was given ten pitches and got three hits, all of them grounders to the right side. One grounder kicked up into the face of a kid trying to field the ball. The kid tried to hang tough as he trotted off the field, head bowed, but Jesse knew tears were welling up in his eyes.

Jesse handed the bat to the next kid and went to sit in the bleachers to wait for the ten-year-olds to bat. He was feeling better than after that morning's fielding tryout because he had gotten three hits. He also thought he looked strong standing at the plate, bat high over his shoulder.

Michael came up to the plate and hit the first pitch to third base. He sent the next pitch into left field. He talked to himself as he stood in the box, bouncing slightly before the next pitch, which he smacked into the outfield. The coach marked his clipboard.

After his ten hits, he jogged off the field and joined his brother in the bleachers. His mouth was again fat from holding back a smile. Jesse was jealous of his brother's athletic display. He thought to himself, Yeah, he'll make the team, and I'll just watch from the bleachers. He imagined Michael running home with a uniform under his arm while he walked home empty-handed.

They watched other kids come to the plate and whack, foul, chop, slice, dribble, and hook balls all over the field.

When a foul ball bounced into the bleachers, Jesse got it. He weighed the ball in his palm, like a pound of bologna, and then hurled it back onto the field. An uninterested coach watched it roll by his feet.

After it was over, they were told to expect a phone call by the end of the week if they had made the team.

By Monday afternoon they were already anxious for the phone to ring. They slouched in the living room after school and watched "Double Dare" on TV. Every time Jesse went into the kitchen, he stole a glance at the telephone. Once, when no one was looking, he picked it up to see if it was working and heard a long buzz.

By Friday, when it was clear the call would never come, they went outside to the front yard to play catch and practice bunting.

"I should have made the team," Michael said as he made a stab at Jesse's bunt. Jesse agreed with him. If anyone should have made the team, it should have been his brother. He was the best one there.

They hit grounders to each other. A few popped off Jesse's chest, but most disappeared neatly into his glove. Why couldn't I do this last Saturday? he wondered. He grew angry at himself, then sad. They stopped playing and returned inside to watch "Double Dare."

Michael and Jesse didn't make Little League that year, but Pete, a friend from school, told them about a team of kids from their school that practiced at Hobo Park near downtown. After school Michael and Jesse raced to the park. They laid their bikes on the grass and took the field. Michael ran to the outfield, and Jesse took second base to practice grounders.

"Give me a baby roller," Danny Lopez, the third baseman, called. Jesse sidearmed a roller, which Danny picked up on the third bounce. "Good pickup," Jesse yelled. Danny looked pleased, slapping his glove against his pants as he hustled back to third.

Michael practiced catching pop-ups with Billy Reeves until Manuel, the coach, arrived in his pickup. Most of the kids ran to let him know they wanted to play first, to play second, to hit first, to hit third. Michael and Jesse were quiet and stood back from the racket.

Manuel pulled a duffel bag from the back of his pickup and walked over to the palm tree that served as a backstop. He dropped the bag with a grunt, clapped his hands, and told the kids to take the field.

The two brothers didn't move. When Pete told the coach that Michael and Jesse wanted to play, Jesse stiffened up and tried to look strong. Because he was older, and wiser, Michael stood with his arms crossed over his chest.

"You guys are in the outfield," the coach shouted before turning to pull a bat and a ball from the bag.

Manuel was middle-aged, patient, and fatherly. He bent down on his haunches to talk to the kids, spoke softly and listened to what they had to say. He cooed "Good" when they made catches, even routine ones. The kids knew he was good to them because most of them didn't have fathers, or had fathers who were so beaten from hard work that they came home and fell asleep in front of the TV set.

The team practiced for two weeks before Manuel announced their first game.

"Who we playing?" asked Pete.

"The Red Caps," he answered. "West Fresno kids."

"What's our name?" two kids asked.

"The Hobos," the coach said, smiling.

In two weeks Jesse had gotten better. But Michael quit the team because he found a girlfriend, a slow walker who hugged her books against her chest while gazing dreamily into Michael's equally dazed face. What fools, Jesse thought as he rode off to practice.

Jesse was catcher and winced behind his mask when the batter swung, because he had no chest protector or shin guards. Balls skidded off his arms and chest, but he never let on that they hurt.

His batting, however, did not improve, and the team knew he was a sure out. Some of the older kids tried to give him tips: how to stand, follow through, and push his weight into the ball. Still, when he came up to bat, the outfielders moved in, like wolves moving in for the kill.

Before their first game, some of the team members met early at Hobo Park to talk about how they were going to whip the Red Caps and send them home crying to their mothers. Soon, others showed up to field grounders while they waited for the coach. When they spotted him, they ran to his pickup and climbed the sides. The coach stuck his head from the cab and warned them to be careful. He waited for a few minutes for the slow kids, and waved for them to get in the front with him. As the team drove slowly to the West Side, the wind running through their hair, they thought they looked pretty neat.

When they arrived, they leaped from the pickup and stood by the coach, who waved to the other coach as he hoisted his duffel bag onto his shoulder. Jesse scanned the other team: most were Mexican like his team, but they had a few blacks.

The coach shook hands with the other coach. They talked quietly in Spanish, then roared with laughter and patted each other's shoulder. They turned around and furrowed their brows at the infield, which was muddy from a recent rain.

Jesse and Pete warmed up behind the backstop, throwing gently to each other and trying to stay calm. Jesse envied the Red Caps, who seemed bigger and scarier than his team and wore matching T-shirts and caps. His team wore jeans and mismatched T-shirts.

The Hobos batted first and scored one run on an error and a double to left field. Then the Red Caps batted and scored four runs on three errors. On the last one, Jesse stood in front of the plate, mask in hand, yelling, "I got a play! I got a play!" But the ball sailed over his head. By the time Jesse picked up the ball, the runner was already sitting on the bench, breathing hard and smiling. Jesse carried the ball to the pitcher.

He searched his face and saw that Elias was scared. "C'mon, you can do it," Jesse said, putting his arm around the pitcher's shoulder. He walked back to the plate. He was wearing a chest protector that reached almost to his knees and made him feel important.

The Red Caps failed to score any more that inning.

In their second turn at bat, the Hobos scored twice on a hit and an error that hurt the Red Caps' catcher. But by the sixth inning, the Red Caps were ahead, sixteen to nine.

The Hobos began arguing with each other. Their play was sloppy, nothing like the cool routines back at their own field. Fly balls to the outfield dropped at the feet of open-mouthed players. Grounders rolled slowly between their legs. Even the pitching stank.

"You *had* to mess up, *menso*," Danny Lopez shouted at the shortstop.

"Well, you didn't get a hit, and *I* did," the shortstop said, pointing to his chest.

From the dugout, the coach told them to be quiet when they started cussing.

Jesse came up to bat for the fourth time that afternoon with two men on and two outs. His teammates moaned because they were sure he was going to strike out or hit a pop-up. To make matters worse, the Red Caps had a new pitcher and he was throwing hard.

Jesse was almost as scared of the pitcher's fast ball as he was of failing. The coach clung to the fence, cooing words of encouragement. His team yelled at Jesse to swing hard. Dig in, they shouted, and he dug in, bat held high over his shoulder. After two balls and a strike, the pitcher threw low and hard toward Jesse's thigh. Jesse stood still because he knew that was the only way he was going to get on base.

The ball hit with a thud, and he went down holding his leg and trying to hold back the tears. The coach ran from the dugout and bent over him, rubbing his leg. A few of the kids on his team came over to ask, "Does it hurt?" "Can I play catcher now?" and "Let me run for him, coach!"

Jesse rose and limped to first. The coach shooed the team back into the dugout and jogged to the coach's box at first. Although his leg hurt, Jesse was happy to be on base. He grinned, looked up, and adjusted his cap. So this is what it's like, he thought. He clapped his hands and encouraged the next batter, their lead-off man. "C'mon, baby, c'mon, you can do it!" The batter hit a high fly ball to deep center. While the outfielder backpedaled and made the catch, Jesse rounded second on his way to third, feeling wonderful to have gotten that far.

Hobo Park lost, nineteen to eleven, and went on to lose against the Red Caps four more times that season. The Hobos were stuck in a two-team league.

Jesse played until the league ended. Fewer and fewer of the players came to practice and the team began using girls to fill in the gaps. One day Manuel didn't show up with his duffel bag. On that day, it was clear to the four boys who remained that the baseball season was over. They threw the ball around, then got on their bikes and rode home. Jesse didn't show up the next day for practice. Instead he sat in front of the TV watching Superman bend iron bars.

He felt guilty though. He thought that one of the guys might have gone to practice and discovered no one there. If he had, he might have waited on the bench or, restless for something to do, he might have practiced pop-ups by throwing the ball into the air, calling, "I got it! I got it!" all by himself.

TWO DREAMERS

Hector's grandfather Luis Molina was born in the small town of Jalapa, but left Mexico to come to the United States when he was in his late twenties. Often, during quiet summer days, he sat in his backyard and remembered his hometown with its clip-clop of horse and donkey hooves, its cleanliness and dusty twilights, the crickets, and the night sky studded with stars. He also remembered his father, a barber who enjoyed listening to his radio, and his mother, who wore flower-print dresses and loved card games.

But that was many years ago, in the land of childhood. Now he lived in Fresno, on a shady street with quiet homes. He had five children, more grandchildren than he had fingers and toes, and was a night watchman at Sun-Maid Raisin.

Luis's favorite grandson was Hector, who was like himself, dreamy and quiet. After work, Luis would sleep until noon, shower, and sit down to his *comida*. Hector, who spent summers with his grandparents, would join Grandfather at the table and watch him eat plates of *frijoles* with *guisado de carne* smothered in chili.

Luis and Hector never said much at the table. It wasn't until his grandfather was finished and sitting in his favorite chair that Hector would begin asking him questions about the world, questions like, "What do Egyptians look like? Is the world really round like a ball? How come we eat chickens and they don't eat us?"

By the time Hector was nine, it was the grandfather who was asking the questions. He had become interested in real estate since he heard that by selling a house his son-in-law had made enough money to buy a brand-new car and put a brick fence around his yard. It impressed him that a young man like Genaro could buy one house, wait a month or two, sell it, and make enough to buy a car and build a brick fence.

After lunch the grandfather would beckon his grandson to come sit with him. *"Ven,* Hector. Come. I want to talk to you. *Quiero hablar contigo."*

They would sit near the window in silence until the grandfather would sigh and begin questioning his grandson. "How much do you think that house is worth? *Mucho dinero,* no? A lot?"

"Grandfather, you asked me that question yesterday," Hector would say, craning his neck to look at the house. It was the yellow one whose porch light was kept on night and day.

"Yes, but that was yesterday. Yesterday I had five dollars in my pocket and now I have only three. Things change, *hijo. Entiendes?*"

Hector stared at the house a long time before making a wild guess. "Thirty thousand?"

"Do you really think so, my boy?" His grandfather would go dreamy with hope. If that house was worth thirty thousand, then his own house, which was better kept and recently painted, would be worth much more. And in Mexico, even thirty thousand dollars would buy a lot of houses. It was his hope that after he retired, he and his wife would return to Mexico, to Jalapa, where all the people would look on them with respect. Not one day would pass without the butcher or barber or pharmacist or ambitious children with dollar signs in their eyes waving to *"El Millonario."*

One day after lunch his grandfather told Hector they were going to go see a house.

"What house?"

Hector's grandmother, who was wiping the table, scolded, *"Viejo, estás chiflado,* you're crazy. Why do you want to buy a house when you already have one?"

The old man ignored her and went to the bathroom to splash cologne on his face and comb his hair. Gently prodding Hector in front of him, he left his house to see another house two blocks away.

Hector and his grandfather stopped in front of a pink house with a "For Sale" sign. The old man took a pencil and little notepad from his shirt pocket and asked Hector to write down the telephone number.

The grandfather paced off the length of the house along the sidewalk and noted the cracks in the stucco.

"Está bonita, no?" he asked Hector.

"I guess so."

"Claro que está bonita, son. Of course it's pretty. And it's probably not so much money, *no crees?"*

"I guess. If you think so."

"How much, do you think?"

"I don't know."

"Sure you do. *A ver, dime."*

"Thirty thousand?"

"Thirty thousand? Do you think so?" His grandfather ran his hand slowly along the stubble of his jaw. Perhaps he could buy it. Perhaps he could put down eight thousand dollars, his life savings, and pay a little each month. He could repaint the house, put up a wrought-iron fence, and plant a lemon tree under the front window. He would also put in a redwood tree that would grow tall and dark so people driving on his street would see it and know Luis Salvador Molina lived in that beautiful house.

Later, while his grandmother was shopping at Hanoian's supermarket, his grandfather prodded Hector to pick up the phone and call the number. Hector, uncomfortable about talking to a grown-up, especially one who sold things, refused to get involved. He went out to the backyard to play fetch with Bon-Bon, his grandmother's poodle. His grandfather followed him into the yard and fiddled with his tomato plants. Finally, he walked over to Hector and said, "I'll give you two dollars."

Thinking it was a pretty good deal, Hector left the poodle sitting up on its hind legs and holding a slobbery tennis ball in his mouth. Hector followed his anxious grand-father inside the house.

"Son, just ask how much. *Es no problema,*" his grand-father assured him. Hector dialed the number with a clumsy finger.

He held his breath as the phone on the other end began to ring. Then there was a click and a voice saying, "Sunny Days Realty." Before the person could ask, May I help you, Hector, who felt faint and was having second thoughts about whether the phone call was worth two dol-lars, asked, "How much?"

"What?"

"How much money?" Hector repeated, cradling the phone nervously in both hands.

"Which property are you speaking of?" The lady seemed calm. Her voice was like the voice of his teacher, which scared Hector because she knew all the answers, more answers about the world than his grandfather, who knew a lot.

"It's a pink one on Orange Street."

"Please hold, and I'll look up that information."

Hector looked at his grandfather, who was combing his hair in the hallway mirror. "She's checking on the house."

After a minute, the woman came back. "That address is six forty-three South Orange, a charming little house. Two bedrooms, large yard, with appliances, and the owners are willing to carry, with a substantial down payment. The house also comes with—"

But Hector, his hands clenched tightly around the tele-phone, interrupted her and asked, "How much?"

There was a moment of silence. Then the woman said, "Forty-three thousand. The owners are anxious and perhaps may settle for less, maybe forty-one five."

"Wait a minute," he said to the woman. Hector looked up to his grandfather. "She says forty-three thousand."

His grandfather groaned and his dream went out like a lightbulb. He put his comb in his back pocket.

"You said thirty thousand, Son."

"I didn't know—I was just guessing."

"But it's so much. *Es demasiado.*"

"Well, I didn't know."

"But you go to school and know about things."

Hector looked at the telephone in his hand. Why did he have to listen to his grandfather and call a person he didn't even know? He was conscious of his grandfather groaning at his side and of a woman's gnat-like voice coming from the telephone, asking, "Would you like to see the house? I can arrange it this afternoon, at two perhaps. And please, may I have your name?"

Hector placed the receiver to his ear and bluntly said, "It costs too much money."

"May I have your name?"

"I'm calling for my grandfather."

His grandfather put a finger before his mouth and let out a *"Sshhhh."* He didn't want to let her know who he was for fear that she would call him later and his wife would scold him for pretending to be a big shot like their son-in-law, Genaro. He took the receiver from Hector and hung up.

Hector didn't bother to ask for his two dollars. He went outside and played fetch with Bon-Bon until his grandmother came home, a bulky grocery bag in her arms. He carried it into the house for her and snuck a peek at his grandfather, who was playing solitaire on a TV tray near the window. He didn't seem disturbed. His face was long and cool, and his eyes were no longer filled with the excitement of money.

While his grandmother started dinner, Hector slouched on the couch reading a comic book until his grandfather whispered, "Hector, come here."

Hector looked over his comic book. His grandfather's eyes once again had that moist wildness of wealth and pink houses. He got up and said loudly, "What do you want, Grandpa?"

"Sshhhh," the old man said, pulling him close. "I want you to call and ask how come the stucco has cracks and why so much money."

"I don't want to," Hector said, trying to pull away from his grandfather's grip.

"Listen, I'll give you something very, very special. It'll be worth a lot of money, Son, when you are old. Now it's only worth some money, but later it will be worth *mucho dinero.*" He whistled and waved his hand. "Lots of money, my boy."

"I don't know, Grandfather, I'm scared."

"Yes, but, you know, you are going to be a rich man, Son."

"What are you going to give me?"

His grandfather rose, pulled his coin purse from his pants pocket, and took a thousand-dollar Confederate bill from a secret fold in his purse. The bill was green, large, and had a picture of a soldier with a long beard.

Hector was impressed. He had seen his grandfather's collection of old bottles and photographs, but this was new. He bit his lower lip and said, "OK."

His grandfather tiptoed to the telephone and stretched the cord into the hallway, away from the kitchen. "Now, you call, and remember to ask how come the cracks, *¿y por qué cuesta tanto?,* how come it costs so much?"

Hector was beginning to sweat. His grandmother was in the next room, and if she caught them trying to be big-shot land barons, she would scold both of them. Grandfather would get the worst of it, of course. The bickering would never end between the two.

He dialed, waited two rings, and heard a man say, "Sunny Days Realty."

"I want to talk to the woman."

"Woman?" the salesman asked.

"The lady. I called her a while ago about the pink house."

Without another word, he put Hector on hold. Hector looked at his grandfather, who was watching out for his wife. "He put us on hold."

The phone clicked and the woman came on. "May I help you?"

"Yeah. I called you about the pink house, remember?"

"Yes. Why did you hang up?"

"My grandfather hung up, not me."

"Well, then, how can I be of help?" Her voice seemed to snap at Hector.

"My grandfather wants to know why the house has so many cracks and how come it's so expensive?"

"What?"

"My grandfather said he seen cracks."

Just then the grandmother's insistent voice rang out: *"Viejo, dónde andas?* I want you to open this bottle."

Terror filled their eyes. Grandfather hung up the phone as the woman was asking, in that faint gnat of a voice, "What in the world are you talking about?"

"Viejo, what are you doing?"

Hector wanted to hide inside the hall closet but knew it was stuffed with coats and the ironing board. Instead, he bent down and pretended to tie his shoe. His grandfather stared at the mirror and began combing his hair.

Grandmother came into the hallway with a jar of *nopales.* She wrinkled her brow and asked, "What are you *locos* doing?"

"Nada," they said in unison.

"You two are up to something. Your faces are dirty with shame." She looked at the phone as if it were a thing she had never seen before and asked, "What is this doing here? You calling a girlfriend, *viejo?"*

"No, no, *viejita.* I don't know how it got here." He shrugged his shoulders and whispered softly to Hector, "Four dollars." Then, in a loud voice, he said, "Do you know, *hijo?"*

Hector was glad to save his grandfather from a scolding that would go on for years. "Oh, I was calling my friend Alfonso about coming over to play."

She eyed both of them. *"Mentirosos!"*

"Es verdad, mi vida," the grandfather said. "It's true. I heard him call his friend. He said, 'Alfonso, come over and play.' "

"Yeah, Grandma."

They argued, but the grandmother finally let them off the hook. They were glad to open the jar of *nopales* and delighted to go out, at the grandmother's suggestion, to mow the lawn before dinner.

Hector and his grandfather mowed with gusto, sweating up a dark storm in the folds of their armpits. They even went down on their knees to clip bunches of grass the mower had missed.

Hector was reluctant to ask his grandfather for the four dollars, but as he swept the driveway and sidewalk, he began to think that maybe his grandfather did owe him the money. He did call the lady, he argued with himself, not once but twice. It wasn't his fault the house cost too much money. As they were finishing up, Hector asked, "How about my four dollars?"

His grandfather, who was pushing the mower into the garage, pursed his lips and thought for a moment. "What is money to a young man like you?" he said finally. "You have no needs, do you?"

"I want my money!"

"What money?"

"You know what I mean. I'm going to tell Grandma."

"Son, I was just kidding." The last thing he wanted was his wife nagging him over dinner. He dug into his coin purse and brought out eight quarters.

"This is only two dollars," Hector complained.

"Yes, but you get the rest when I buy the pink house. You wait, Son, you'll be a rich man one of these days. One day it will all be yours."

Hector didn't say anything. He was glad to have the money and even gladder that his grandmother didn't scold them. After setting the sprinkler on the lawn, the two hardworking men went in for dinner.

BARBIE

The day after Christmas, Veronica Solis and her baby sister, Yolanda, nestled together on the couch to watch the morning cartoons. Bumbling Inspector Gadget was in trouble again, unaware that the edge of the cliff was crumbling under his feet. Soon he was sliding down the mountain toward a pit of alligators. He commanded, "Go, go, gadget umbrella," and a red umbrella popped out of his hat. He landed safely just a few feet from a dark green alligator and dusted himself off.

Veronica liked this show, but she was really waiting for the next one: "My Little Pony." That show had lots of Barbie commercials and Veronica was in love with Barbie, her blond hair, her slim waist and long legs, and the glamorous clothes on tiny hangers. She had wanted a Barbie for as long as she could remember and almost got one last Christmas, but her Uncle Rudy, who had more money than all her other uncles combined, bought her the worst kind of doll, an imitation Barbie.

Veronica had torn the silver wrapping off her gift and found a black-haired doll with a flat, common nose, not like Barbie's cute, upturned nose. She had wanted to cry, but she gave her uncle a hug, forced a smile, and went to her bedroom to stare at the doll. A tear slid down her cheek.

"You ugly thing," she snapped and threw the imposter against the wall. The doll lay on the floor, eyes open like the dead. Immediately, Veronica felt ashamed. She picked up the doll and set it beside her.

"I'm sorry. I don't hate you," she whispered. "It's just that you're not a *real* Barbie." She noticed that the forehead was chipped where it had struck the wall, and that one of the eyelashes was peeling off like a scab.

"Oh, no," she gasped. Veronica tried to push the eyelash back into place, but it came off and stuck to her thumb. "Doggone it," she mumbled and returned to the living room, where her uncle was singing Mexican Christmas songs.

He stopped to sip from his coffee cup and pat Veronica's hand. "Did you name your doll yet?"

"No, not yet." Veronica looked at the floor. She hoped that he wouldn't ask her to bring it out.

"Let's see her. I'll sing her a song," he teased.

Veronica didn't want him to see that the doll's face was chipped and one of her eyelashes was gone.

"She's asleep," she said.

"Well, in that case, we'll let her sleep," he said. "I'll sing her a lullaby, 'Rock-a-Bye-Baby' in Spanish."

That was last year. There had been no Barbie this Christmas either. Today was just a cold, winter morning in front of the television.

Her Uncle Rudy came over to the house with his girlfriend, Donna. Veronica's mother was uneasy. Why was the girlfriend here? Was this the moment? She dried her hands on a kitchen towel and told the children to go play outside. She turned to the woman and, ignoring her brother, asked, "What'd you get for Christmas?"

"A robe and slippers," she said, looking at Rudy, then added, "and a sweatsuit from my brother."

"Come, have a seat. I'll start coffee."

"Helen, would you call Veronica back inside?" Rudy asked. "We have an extra present for her."

"OK," she said, hurrying to the kitchen, her face worried because something was up and it could be marriage. She called, "Veronica, your uncle wants you."

Veronica dropped her end of the jump rope, leaving her sister and brother to carry on without her. She walked back into the house and stood by her uncle; but she couldn't take her eyes off the woman.

"How's school?" asked her uncle.

"Fine," she said shyly.

"Getting good grades?"

"Pretty good."

"As good as the boys? Better?"

"Lots better."

"Any *novios?*"

Donna slapped Rudy's arm playfully. "Rudy, quit teasing the child. Give it to her."

"OK," he said, patting Donna's hand. He turned to Veronica. "I have something for you. Something I know you wanted."

Uncle Rudy's girlfriend reached in a package at her feet and brought out a Barbie doll in a striped, one-piece swimsuit. "This is for you, honey."

Veronica stared at the woman, then at the doll. The woman's eyes were almost as blue, and her hair almost as blond as Barbie's. Veronica slowly took the Barbie from the woman and very softly said, "Thank you." She gave her uncle a big hug, taking care not to smash Barbie against his chest. Veronica smiled at the woman, then at her mother, who returned from the kitchen with a pot of coffee and a plate of powdery-white donuts.

"Look, Mom, a Barbie," Veronica said happily.

"Oh, Rudy, you're spoiling this girl," Mrs. Solis chided.

"And that's not all," Rudy said. "Donna, show her the clothes."

The woman brought out three outfits: a summer dress, a pants suit, and a lacy gown the color of mother-of-pearl.

"They're lovely!" said the mother. She held the summer dress up and laughed at how tiny it was.

"I like them a lot," said Veronica. "It's just like on TV."

The grown-ups sipped their coffee and watched Veronica inspect the clothes. After a few minutes Rudy sat up and cleared his throat.

"I have something to say," he said to his sister, who already suspected what it was. "We're getting married—soon."

He patted Donna's hand, which sported a sparkling ring, and announced a second time that he and Donna were getting married. The date wasn't set yet, but they would have their wedding in the spring. Veronica's mother, feigning surprise, lifted her eyes and said, "Oh, how wonderful! Oh, Rudy—and Donna." She kissed her brother and the woman.

"Did you hear, Veronica? Your uncle is going to get married." She hesitated, then added, "To Donna."

Veronica pretended to look happy, but she was too preoccupied with her new doll.

In her bedroom Veronica hugged her Barbie and told her she was beautiful. She combed Barbie's hair with a tiny blue comb and dressed her in the three outfits. She made believe that Barbie was on a lunch date with a girlfriend from work, the fake Barbie with the chipped forehead and missing eyelash.

"Oh, look—boys!" the ugly doll said. "They're so cute."

"Oh, those boys," Barbie said coolly. "They're OK, but Ken is so much more handsome. And richer."

"They're good-looking to me. I'm not as pretty as you, Barbie."

"That's true," Barbie said. "But I still like you. How's your sandwich?"

"Good, but not as good as your sandwich," the ugly doll answered.

Veronica was eager to make Barbie the happiest person in the world. She dressed her in her swimsuit and said in a fake English accent, "You look smashing, my child."

"And who are you going to marry?" the fake Barbie asked.

"The king," she announced. Veronica raised Barbie's movable arms. "The king is going to buy me a yacht and build me a swimming pool." Veronica made Barbie dive into an imaginary pool. "The king loves me more than money. He would die for me."

Veronica played in her room all afternoon, and the next day called her friend Martha. Martha had two Barbies and one Ken. She invited Veronica to come over to play Barbies, and play they did. The three Barbies went to Disneyland and Magic Mountain and ate at an expensive restaurant where they talked about boys. Then all three took turns kissing Ken.

"Ken, you kiss too hard," Martha giggled.

"You forgot to shave," whined Veronica.

"Sorry," Ken said.

"That's better," they said, laughing, and clacked the dolls' faces together.

But at the end of the day the two girls got into an argument when Martha tried to switch the Barbies so she would get Veronica's newer Barbie. Veronica saw that Martha was trying to trick her and pushed her against the bureau, yelling, "You stupid cheater!" She left with her three outfits and Barbie under her arm.

At the corner she hugged and kissed Barbie. "That's the last time we're going to her house," said Veronica. "She almost stole you."

She sat on the curb, dressed Barbie in her pants suit, then walked through an alley where she knew there was an orange tree. She stopped under the tree, which was heavy with oranges the size of softballs, and swiped one.

As she walked home she peeled the orange with her polish-chipped nails and looked around the neighborhood. With her Barbie doll pressed under her arm, she was happy. The day was almost over, and soon she and Barbie would be sitting down to dinner. After she finished the orange, she wiped her hands on her pants and started to play with Barbie.

"Oh, it's a beautiful day to look pretty," Barbie said. "Yes, I'm going to—"

Veronica stopped in midsentence. Barbie's head was gone. Veronica waved her hand over the space where a smile and blond hair had been only a few minutes ago.

"Darn it," she hissed. "Her head's gone."

She fell to one knee and felt around. She picked up ragged leaves, loose dirt, and bottle caps. "Where is it?" She checked the leaf-choked gutter and raked her hand through the weeds along a fence. She slowly retraced her steps into the alley, desperately scanning the ground. She looked at the headless Barbie in her hand. She wanted to cry but knew it would just make her eyes blurry.

"Where are you?" Veronica called to the head. "Please let me find you."

She came to the orange tree. She got down and searched on all fours, but found nothing. She pounded the ground with her fists and burst into tears.

"She's ruined," Veronica sobbed. "Oh, Barbie, look at you. You're no good anymore." She looked through her tears at Barbie and got mad. How could Barbie do this to her after only one day?

For the next hour she searched the street and the alley. She even knocked on Martha's door and asked her if she had seen Barbie's head.

"No," Martha said. She kept the door half-closed because she was afraid that Veronica was still mad at her for trying to switch their Barbies. "Did you lose it?"

"It just fell off. I don't know what happened. It was brand-new."

"How did it fall off?"

"How do I know? It just fell off. Stupid thing!"

Veronica looked so distressed that Martha went outside and helped her look, assuring Veronica that together they would find the head.

"One time I lost my bike keys at the playground," Martha said. "I just looked and looked. I just got on my knees and crawled around. Nobody helped me. I found them all by myself."

Veronica ignored Martha's chatter. She was busy parting weeds with her hands and overturning rocks and boards under which the head might have rolled. After a while Veronica had a hard time concentrating and had to keep reminding herself what she was looking for. "Head," she said, "look for the head." But everything became jumbled together. She stared at the ground so long that she couldn't tell an eggshell from a splintered squirt gun.

If only it could talk, wished Veronica, who was once again on the verge of tears. If only it could yell, "Over here, I'm here by the fence. Come and get me." She blamed herself, then Martha. If they hadn't had that argument, everything would have been all right. She would have played and then returned home. She probably jinxed her Barbie when she pushed Martha against the chest of drawers. Maybe that was when Barbie's head had come loose; she had been holding Barbie while she fought Martha.

When it began to get dark Martha said she had to go. "But I'll help you tomorrow if you want," she said.

Veronica puckered her mouth and shouted, "It's all your fault! You made me mad. You tried to cheat me. My Barbie was more beautiful than yours, and now see what you've done!" She held the headless Barbie up for Martha to see. Martha turned away and ran.

That night Veronica sat in her room. She felt that she had betrayed Barbie by not caring for her and couldn't stand to look at her. She wanted to tell her mother, but she knew Mom would scold her for being a *mensa*.

"If only I could tell Uncle Rudy's girlfriend," she said. "She would understand. She would do something."

Finally, Veronica dressed in her nightie, brushed her teeth, and jumped into bed. She started reading a library book about a girl in New York City who had lost her cat, but tossed it aside because the words on the page meant nothing. It was a made-up story, while her own sadness was real.

"I shouldn't have gone," said Veronica, staring at the ceiling. "I should have stayed home and played by myself."

She sat up and tried to read again, but she couldn't concentrate. She picked at a scab on her wrist and tried to lull herself to sleep with sad thoughts. When she couldn't stand it anymore, she kicked off the blankets and walked over to her Barbie, which lay on a chest of drawers. She picked up the fake Barbie, too.

"Let's go to sleep," she whispered to both dolls, and carried them lovingly to bed.

THE NO-GUITAR
BLUES

The moment Fausto saw the group Los Lobos on "American Bandstand," he knew exactly what he wanted to do with his life—play guitar. His eyes grew large with excitement as Los Lobos ground out a song while teenagers bounced off each other on the crowded dance floor.

He had watched "American Bandstand" for years and had heard Ray Camacho and the Teardrops at Romain Playground, but it had never occurred to him that he too might become a musician. That afternoon Fausto knew his mission in life: to play guitar in his own band; to sweat out his songs and prance around the stage; to make money and dress weird.

Fausto turned off the television set and walked outside,

wondering how he could get enough money to buy a guitar. He couldn't ask his parents because they would just say, "Money doesn't grow on trees" or "What do you think we are, bankers?" And besides, they hated rock music. They were into the *conjunto* music of Lydia Mendoza, Flaco Jimenez, and Little Joe and La Familia. And, as Fausto recalled, the last album they bought was *The Chipmunks Sing Christmas Favorites.*

But what the heck, he'd give it a try. He returned inside and watched his mother make tortillas. He leaned against the kitchen counter, trying to work up the nerve to ask her for a guitar. Finally, he couldn't hold back any longer.

"Mom," he said, "I want a guitar for Christmas."

She looked up from rolling tortillas. "Honey, a guitar costs a lot of money."

"How 'bout for my birthday next year," he tried again.

"I can't promise," she said, turning back to her tortillas, "but we'll see."

Fausto walked back outside with a buttered tortilla. He knew his mother was right. His father was a warehouseman at Berven Rugs, where he made good money but not enough to buy everything his children wanted. Fausto decided to mow lawns to earn money, and was pushing the mower down the street before he realized it was winter and no one would hire him. He returned the mower and picked up a rake. He hopped onto his sister's bike (his had two flat tires) and rode north to the nicer section of Fresno in search of work. He went door-to-door, but after three hours he managed to get only one job, and not to rake leaves. He was asked to hurry down to the store to buy a loaf of bread, for which he received a grimy, dirt-caked quarter.

He also got an orange, which he ate sitting at the curb. While he was eating, a dog walked up and sniffed his leg. Fausto pushed him away and threw an orange peel skyward. The dog caught it and ate it in one gulp. The dog looked at Fausto and wagged his tail for more. Fausto tossed him a slice of orange, and the dog snapped it up and licked his lips.

"How come you like oranges, dog?"

The dog blinked a pair of sad eyes and whined.

"What's the matter? Cat got your tongue?" Fausto laughed at his joke and offered the dog another slice.

At that moment a dim light came on inside Fausto's head. He saw that it was sort of a fancy dog, a terrier or something, with dog tags and a shiny collar. And it looked well fed and healthy. In his neighborhood, the dogs were never licensed, and if they got sick they were placed near the water heater until they got well.

This dog looked like he belonged to rich people. Fausto cleaned his juice-sticky hands on his pants and got to his feet. The light in his head grew brighter. It just might work. He called the dog, patted its muscular back, and bent down to check the license.

"Great," he said. "There's an address."

The dog's name was Roger, which struck Fausto as weird because he'd never heard of a dog with a human name. Dogs should have names like Bomber, Freckles, Queenie, Killer, and Zero.

Fausto planned to take the dog home and collect a reward. He would say he had found Roger near the freeway. That would scare the daylights out of the owners, who would be so happy that they would probably give him a reward. He felt bad about lying, but the dog *was* loose. And it might even really be lost, because the address was six blocks away.

Fausto stashed the rake and his sister's bike behind a bush, and, tossing an orange peel every time Roger became distracted, walked the dog to his house. He hesitated on the porch until Roger began to scratch the door with a muddy paw. Fausto had come this far, so he figured he might as well go through with it. He knocked softly. When no one answered, he rang the doorbell. A man in a silky bathrobe and slippers opened the door and seemed confused by the sight of his dog and the boy.

"Sir," Fausto said, gripping Roger by the collar. "I found your dog by the freeway. His dog license says he lives here." Fausto looked down at the dog, then up to the man. "He does, doesn't he?"

The man stared at Fausto a long time before saying in a pleasant voice, "That's right." He pulled his robe tighter around him because of the cold and asked Fausto to come in. "So he was by the freeway?"

"Uh-huh."

"You bad, snoopy dog," said the man, wagging his finger. "You probably knocked over some trash cans, too, didn't you?"

Fausto didn't say anything. He looked around, amazed by this house with its shiny furniture and a television as large as the front window at home. Warm bread smells filled the air and music full of soft tinkling floated in from another room.

"Helen," the man called to the kitchen. "We have a visitor." His wife came into the living room wiping her hands on a dish towel and smiling. "And who have we here?" she asked in one of the softest voices Fausto had ever heard.

"This young man said he found Roger near the freeway."

Fausto repeated his story to her while staring at a perpetual clock with a bell-shaped glass, the kind his aunt got when she celebrated her twenty-fifth anniversary. The lady frowned and said, wagging a finger at Roger, "Oh, you're a bad boy."

"It was very nice of you to bring Roger home," the man said. "Where do you live?"

"By that vacant lot on Olive," he said. "You know, by Brownie's Flower Place."

The wife looked at her husband, then Fausto. Her eyes twinkled triangles of light as she said, "Well, young man, you're probably hungry. How about a turnover?"

"What do I have to turn over?" Fausto asked, thinking she was talking about yard work or something like turning trays of dried raisins.

"No, no, dear, it's a pastry." She took him by the elbow and guided him to a kitchen that sparkled with copper pans and bright yellow wallpaper. She guided him to the kitchen table and gave him a tall glass of milk and something that looked like an *empanada*. Steamy waves of heat escaped when he tore it in two. He ate with both eyes on the man and woman who stood arm-in-arm smiling at him. They were strange, he thought. But nice.

"That was good," he said after he finished the turnover. "Did you make it, ma'am?"

"Yes, I did. Would you like another?"

"No, thank you. I have to go home now."

As Fausto walked to the door, the man opened his wallet and took out a bill. "This is for you," he said. "Roger is special to us, almost like a son."

Fausto looked at the bill and knew he was in trouble. Not with these nice folks or with his parents but with himself. How could he have been so deceitful? The dog wasn't lost. It was just having a fun Saturday walking around.

"I can't take that."

"You have to. You deserve it, believe me," the man said.

"No, I don't."

"Now don't be silly," said the lady. She took the bill from her husband and stuffed it into Fausto's shirt pocket. "You're a lovely child. Your parents are lucky to have you. Be good. And come see us again, please."

Fausto went out, and the lady closed the door. Fausto clutched the bill through his shirt pocket. He felt like ringing the doorbell and begging them to please take the money back, but he knew they would refuse. He hurried away, and at the end of the block, pulled the bill from his shirt pocket: it was a crisp twenty-dollar bill.

"Oh, man, I shouldn't have lied," he said under his breath as he started up the street like a zombie. He wanted to run to church for Saturday confession, but it was past four-thirty, when confession stopped.

He returned to the bush where he had hidden the rake and his sister's bike and rode home slowly, not daring to touch the money in his pocket. At home, in the privacy of his room, he examined the twenty-dollar bill. He had never had so much money. It was probably enough to buy a secondhand guitar. But he felt bad, like the time he stole a dollar from the secret fold inside his older brother's wallet.

Fausto went outside and sat on the fence. "Yeah," he said. "I can probably get a guitar for twenty. Maybe at a yard sale—things are cheaper."

His mother called him to dinner.

The next day he dressed for church without anyone telling him. He was going to go to eight o'clock mass.

"I'm going to church, Mom," he said. His mother was in the kitchen cooking *papas* and *chorizo con huevos.* A pile of tortillas lay warm under a dishtowel.

"Oh, I'm so proud of you, Son." She beamed, turning over the crackling *papas.*

His older brother, Lawrence, who was at the table reading the funnies, mimicked, "Oh, I'm so proud of you, my son," under his breath.

At Saint Theresa's he sat near the front. When Father Jerry began by saying that we are all sinners, Fausto thought he looked right at him. Could he know? Fausto fidgeted with guilt. No, he thought. I only did it yesterday.

Fausto knelt, prayed, and sang. But he couldn't forget the man and the lady, whose names he didn't even know, and the *empanada* they had given him. It had a strange name but tasted really good. He wondered how they got rich. And how that dome clock worked. He had asked his mother once how his aunt's clock worked. She said it just worked, the way the refrigerator works. It just did.

Fausto caught his mind wandering and tried to concentrate on his sins. He said a Hail Mary and sang, and when the wicker basket came his way, he stuck a hand reluctantly in his pocket and pulled out the twenty-dollar bill. He ironed it between his palms, and dropped it into the basket. The grown-ups stared. Here was a kid dropping twenty dollars in the basket while they gave just three or four dollars.

There would be a second collection for Saint Vincent de Paul, the lector announced. The wicker baskets again floated in the pews, and this time the adults around him, given a second chance to show their charity, dug deep into their wallets and purses and dropped in fives and tens. This time Fausto tossed in the grimy quarter.

Fausto felt better after church. He went home and played football in the front yard with his brother and some neighbor kids. He felt cleared of wrongdoing and was so happy that he played one of his best games of football ever. On one play, he tore his good pants, which he knew he shouldn't have been wearing. For a second, while he examined the hole, he wished he hadn't given the twenty dollars away.

Man, I coulda bought me some Levi's, he thought. He pictured his twenty dollars being spent to buy church candles. He pictured a priest buying an armful of flowers with *his* money.

Fausto had to forget about getting a guitar. He spent the next day playing soccer in his good pants, which were now his old pants. But that night during dinner, his mother said she remembered seeing an old bass guitarron the last time she cleaned out her father's garage.

"It's a little dusty," his mom said, serving his favorite enchiladas, "But I think it works. Grandpa says it works."

Fausto's ears perked up. That was the same kind the guy in Los Lobos played. Instead of asking for the guitar, he waited for his mother to offer it to him. And she did, while gathering the dishes from the table.

"No, Mom, I'll do it," he said, hugging her. "I'll do the dishes forever if you want."

It was the happiest day of his life. No, it was the second-happiest day of his life. The happiest was when his grandfather Lupe placed the guitarron, which was nearly as huge as a washtub, in his arms. Fausto ran a thumb down the strings, which vibrated in his throat and chest. It sounded beautiful, deep and eerie. A pumpkin smile widened on his face.

"OK, *hijo,* now you put your fingers like this," said his grandfather, smelling of tobacco and aftershave. He took Fausto's fingers and placed them on the strings. Fausto strummed a chord on the guitarron, and the bass resounded in their chests.

The guitarron was more complicated than Fausto imagined. But he was confident that after a few more lessons he could start a band that would someday play on "American Bandstand" for the dancing crowds.

SEVENTH GRADE

On the first day of school, Victor stood in line half an hour before he came to a wobbly card table. He was handed a packet of papers and a computer card on which he listed his one elective, French. He already spoke Spanish and English, but he thought some day he might travel to France, where it was cool; not like Fresno, where summer days reached 110 degrees in the shade. There were rivers in France, and huge churches, and fair-skinned people everywhere, the way there were brown people all around Victor.

Besides, Teresa, a girl he had liked since they were in catechism classes at Saint Theresa's, was taking French, too. With any luck they would be in the same class. Teresa is going to be my girl this year, he promised himself as he left the gym full of students in their new fall clothes. She was cute. And good at math, too, Victor thought as he walked down the hall to his homeroom. He ran into his friend, Michael Torres, by the water fountain that never turned off.

They shook hands, *raza*-style, and jerked their heads at one another in a *saludo de vato.* "How come you're making a face?" asked Victor.

"I ain't making a face, *ese.* This *is* my face." Michael said his face had changed during the summer. He had read a *GQ* magazine that his older brother borrowed from the Book Mobile and noticed that the male models all had the same look on their faces. They would stand, one arm around a beautiful woman, and *scowl.* They would sit at a pool, their rippled stomachs dark with shadow, and *scowl.* They would sit at dinner tables, cool drinks in their hands, and *scowl.*

"I think it works," Michael said. He scowled and let his upper lip quiver. His teeth showed along with the ferocity of his soul. "Belinda Reyes walked by a while ago and looked at me," he said.

Victor didn't say anything, though he thought his friend looked pretty strange. They talked about recent movies, baseball, their parents, and the horrors of picking grapes in order to buy their fall clothes. Picking grapes was like living in Siberia, except hot and more boring.

"What classes are you taking?" Michael said, scowling.

"French. How 'bout you?"

"Spanish. I ain't so good at it, even if I'm Mexican."

"I'm not either, but I'm better at it than math, that's for sure."

A tinny, three-beat bell propelled students to their

homerooms. The two friends socked each other in the arm and went their ways, Victor thinking, man, that's weird. Michael thinks making a face makes him handsome.

On the way to his homeroom, Victor tried a scowl. He felt foolish, until out of the corner of his eye he saw a girl looking at him. Umm, he thought, maybe it does work. He scowled with greater conviction.

In homeroom, roll was taken, emergency cards were passed out, and they were given a bulletin to take home to their parents. The principal, Mr. Belton, spoke over the crackling loudspeaker, welcoming the students to a new year, new experiences, and new friendships. The students squirmed in their chairs and ignored him. They were anxious to go to first period. Victor sat calmly, thinking of Teresa, who sat two rows away, reading a paperback novel. This would be his lucky year. She was in his homeroom, and would probably be in his English and math classes. And, of course, French.

The bell rang for first period, and the students herded noisily through the door. Only Teresa lingered, talking with the homeroom teacher.

"So you think I should talk to Mrs. Gaines?" she asked the teacher. "She would know about ballet?"

"She would be a good bet," the teacher said. Then added, "Or the gym teacher, Mrs. Garza."

Victor lingered, keeping his head down and staring at his desk. He wanted to leave when she did so he could bump into her and say something clever.

He watched her on the sly. As she turned to leave, he stood up and hurried to the door, where he managed to catch her eye. She smiled and said, "Hi, Victor."

He smiled back and said, "Yeah, that's me." His brown face blushed. Why hadn't he said, "Hi, Teresa," or "How was your summer?" or something nice?

As Teresa walked down the hall, Victor walked the other way, looking back, admiring how gracefully she walked, one foot in front of the other. So much for being in the same class, he thought. As he trudged to English, he practiced scowling.

In English they reviewed the parts of speech. Mr. Lucas, a portly man, waddled down the aisle, asking, "What is a noun?"

"A person, place, or thing," said the class in unison.

"Yes, now somebody give me an example of a person—you, Victor Rodriguez."

"Teresa," Victor said automatically. Some of the girls giggled. They knew he had a crush on Teresa. He felt himself blushing again.

"Correct," Mr. Lucas said. "Now provide me with a place."

Mr. Lucas called on a freckled kid who answered, "Teresa's house with a kitchen full of big brothers."

After English, Victor had math, his weakest subject. He sat in the back by the window, hoping that he would not be called on. Victor understood most of the problems, but some of the stuff looked like the teacher made it up as she went along. It was confusing, like the inside of a watch.

After math he had a fifteen-minute break, then social studies, and, finally, lunch. He bought a tuna casserole with buttered rolls, some fruit cocktail, and milk. He sat with Michael, who practiced scowling between bites.

Girls walked by and looked at him.

"See what I mean, Vic?" Michael scowled. "They love it."

"Yeah, I guess so."

They ate slowly, Victor scanning the horizon for a glimpse of Teresa. He didn't see her. She must have brought lunch, he thought, and is eating outside. Victor scraped his plate and left Michael, who was busy scowling at a girl two tables away.

The small, triangle-shaped campus bustled with students talking about their new classes. Everyone was in a sunny mood. Victor hurried to the bag lunch area, where he sat down and opened his math book. He moved his lips as if he were reading, but his mind was somewhere else. He raised his eyes slowly and looked around. No Teresa.

He lowered his eyes, pretending to study, then looked slowly to the left. No Teresa. He turned a page in the book and stared at some math problems that scared him because he knew he would have to do them eventually. He looked to the right. Still no sign of her. He stretched out lazily in an attempt to disguise his snooping.

Then he saw her. She was sitting with a girlfriend under a plum tree. Victor moved to a table near her and daydreamed about taking her to a movie. When the bell sounded, Teresa looked up, and their eyes met. She smiled sweetly and gathered her books. Her next class was French, same as Victor's.

They were among the last students to arrive in class, so all the good desks in the back had already been taken. Victor was forced to sit near the front, a few desks away from Teresa, while Mr. Bueller wrote French words on the chalkboard. The bell rang, and Mr. Bueller wiped his hands, turned to the class, and said, *"Bonjour."*

56

"Bonjour," braved a few students.

"Bonjour," Victor whispered. He wondered if Teresa heard him.

Mr. Bueller said that if the students studied hard, at the end of the year they could go to France and be understood by the populace.

One kid raised his hand and asked, "What's 'populace'?"

"The people, the people of France."

Mr. Bueller asked if anyone knew French. Victor raised his hand, wanting to impress Teresa. The teacher beamed and said, *"Très bien. Parlez-vous français?"*

Victor didn't know what to say. The teacher wet his lips and asked something else in French. The room grew silent. Victor felt all eyes staring at him. He tried to bluff his way out by making noises that sounded French.

"La me vava me con le grandma," he said uncertainly.

Mr. Bueller, wrinkling his face in curiosity, asked him to speak up.

Great rosebushes of red bloomed on Victor's cheeks. A river of nervous sweat ran down his palms. He felt awful. Teresa sat a few desks away, no doubt thinking he was a fool. Without looking at Mr. Bueller, Victor mumbled, "Frenchie oh wewe gee in September."

Mr. Bueller asked Victor to repeat what he had said.

"Frenchie oh wewe gee in September," Victor repeated.

Mr. Bueller understood that the boy didn't know French and turned away. He walked to the blackboard and pointed to the words on the board with his steel-edged ruler.

"Le bateau," he sang.

"Le bateau," the students repeated.

"Le bateau est sur l'eau," he sang.

"Le bateau est sur l'eau."

Victor was too weak from failure to join the class. He stared at the board and wished he had taken Spanish, not French. Better yet, he wished he could start his life over. He had never been so embarrassed. He bit his thumb until he tore off a sliver of skin.

The bell sounded for fifth period, and Victor shot out of the room, avoiding the stares of the other kids, but had to return for his math book. He looked sheepishly at the teacher, who was erasing the board, then widened his eyes in terror at Teresa who stood in front of him. "I didn't know you knew French," she said. "That was good."

Mr. Bueller looked at Victor, and Victor looked back. Oh please, don't say anything, Victor pleaded with his eyes. I'll wash your car, mow your lawn, walk your dog—anything! I'll be your best student, and I'll clean your erasers after school.

Mr. Bueller shuffled through the papers on his desk. He smiled and hummed as he sat down to work. He remembered his college years when he dated a girlfriend in borrowed cars. She thought he was rich because each time he picked her up he had a different car. It was fun until he had spent all his money on her and had to write home to his parents because he was broke.

Victor couldn't stand to look at Teresa. He was sweaty with shame. "Yeah, well, I picked up a few things from movies and books and stuff like that." They left the class together. Teresa asked him if he would help her with her French.

"Sure, anytime," Victor said.

"I won't be bothering you, will I?"

"Oh no, I like being bothered."

"Bonjour," Teresa said, leaving him outside her next class. She smiled and pushed wisps of hair from her face.

"Yeah, right, *bonjour,"* Victor said. He turned and headed to his class. The rosebushes of shame on his face became bouquets of love. Teresa is a great girl, he thought. And Mr. Bueller is a good guy.

He raced to metal shop. After metal shop there was biology, and after biology a long sprint to the public library, where he checked out three French textbooks.

He was going to like seventh grade.

MOTHER
AND DAUGHTER

Yollie's mother, Mrs. Moreno, was a large woman who wore a muumuu and butterfly-shaped glasses. She liked to water her lawn in the evening and wave at low-riders, who would stare at her behind their smoky sunglasses and laugh. Now and then a low-rider from Belmont Avenue would make his car jump and shout *"Mamacita!"* But most of the time they just stared and wondered how she got so large.

Mrs. Moreno had a strange sense of humor. Once, Yollie and her mother were watching a late-night movie called "They Came to Look." It was about creatures from the underworld who had climbed through molten lava to walk the earth. But Yollie, who had played soccer all day with the kids next door, was too tired to be scared. Her eyes closed but sprang open when her mother screamed, "Look, Yollie! Oh, you missed a scary part. The guy's face was all ugly!"

But Yollie couldn't keep her eyes open. They fell shut again and stayed shut, even when her mother screamed and slammed a heavy palm on the arm of her chair.

"Mom, wake me up when the movie's over so I can go to bed," mumbled Yollie.

"OK, Yollie, I wake you," said her mother through a mouthful of popcorn.

But after the movie ended, instead of waking her daughter, Mrs. Moreno laughed under her breath, turned the TV and lights off, and tiptoed to bed. Yollie woke up in the middle of the night and didn't know where she was. For a moment she thought she was dead. Maybe something from the underworld had lifted her from her house and carried her into the earth's belly. She blinked her sleepy eyes, looked around at the darkness, and called, "Mom? Mom, where are you?" But there was no answer, just the throbbing hum of the refrigerator.

Finally, Yollie's grogginess cleared and she realized her mother had gone to bed, leaving her on the couch. Another of her little jokes.

But Yollie wasn't laughing. She tiptoed into her mother's bedroom with a glass of water and set it on the nightstand next to the alarm clock. The next morning, Yollie woke to screams. When her mother reached to turn off the alarm, she had overturned the glass of water.

Yollie burned her mother's morning toast and gloated. "Ha! Ha! I got you back. Why did you leave me on the couch when I told you to wake me up?"

Despite their jokes, mother and daughter usually got along. They watched bargain matinees together, and played croquet in the summer and checkers in the winter. Mrs. Moreno encouraged Yollie to study hard because she wanted her daughter to be a doctor. She bought Yollie a desk, a typewriter, and a lamp that cut glare so her eyes would not grow tired from hours of studying.

Yollie was slender as a tulip, pretty, and one of the smartest kids at Saint Theresa's. She was captain of crossing guards, an altar girl, and a whiz in the school's monthly spelling bees.

"Tienes que estudiar mucho," Mrs. Moreno said every time she propped her work-weary feet on the hassock. "You have to study a lot, then you can get a good job and take care of me."

"Yes, Mama," Yollie would respond, her face buried in a book. If she gave her mother any sympathy, she would begin her stories about how she had come with her family from Mexico with nothing on her back but a sack with three skirts, all of which were too large by the time she crossed the border because she had lost weight from not having enough to eat.

Everyone thought Yollie's mother was a riot. Even the nuns laughed at her antics. Her brother Raul, a nightclub owner, thought she was funny enough to go into show business.

But there was nothing funny about Yollie needing a new outfit for the eighth-grade fall dance. They couldn't afford one. It was late October, with Christmas around the corner, and their dented Chevy Nova had gobbled up almost one hundred dollars in repairs.

"We don't have the money," said her mother, genuinely sad because they couldn't buy the outfit, even though there was a little money stashed away for college. Mrs. Moreno remembered her teenage years and her hardworking parents, who picked grapes and oranges, and chopped beets and cotton for meager pay around Kerman. Those were the days when "new clothes" meant limp and out-of-style dresses from Saint Vincent de Paul.

The best Mrs. Moreno could do was buy Yollie a pair of black shoes with velvet bows and fabric dye to color her white summer dress black.

"We can color your dress so it will look brand-new," her mother said brightly, shaking the bottle of dye as she ran hot water into a plastic dish tub. She poured the black liquid into the tub and stirred it with a pencil. Then, slowly and carefully, she lowered the dress into the tub.

Yollie couldn't stand to watch. She *knew* it wouldn't work. It would be like the time her mother stirred up a batch of molasses for candy apples on Yollie's birthday. She'd dipped the apples into the goo and swirled them and seemed to taunt Yollie by singing *"Las Mañanitas"* to her. When she was through, she set the apples on wax paper. They were hard as rocks and hurt the kids' teeth. Finally they had a contest to see who could break the apples open by throwing them against the side of the house. The apples shattered like grenades, sending the kids scurrying for cover, and in an odd way the birthday party turned out to be a success. At least everyone went home happy.

To Yollie's surprise, the dress came out shiny black. It looked brand-new and sophisticated, like what people in New York wear. She beamed at her mother, who hugged Yollie and said, "See, what did I tell you?"

The dance was important to Yollie because she was in

love with Ernie Castillo, the third-best speller in the class. She bathed, dressed, did her hair and nails, and primped until her mother yelled, "All right already." Yollie sprayed her neck and wrists with Mrs. Moreno's Avon perfume and bounced into the car.

Mrs. Moreno let Yollie out in front of the school. She waved and told her to have a good time but behave herself, then roared off, blue smoke trailing from the tail pipe of the old Nova.

Yollie ran into her best friend, Janice. They didn't say it, but each thought the other was the most beautiful girl at the dance; the boys would fall over themselves asking them to dance.

The evening was warm but thick with clouds. Gusts of wind picked up the paper lanterns hanging in the trees and swung them, blurring the night with reds and yellows. The lanterns made the evening seem romantic, like a scene from a movie. Everyone danced, sipped punch, and stood in knots of threes and fours, talking. Sister Kelly got up and jitterbugged with some kid's father. When the record ended, students broke into applause.

Janice had her eye on Frankie Ledesma, and Yollie, who kept smoothing her dress down when the wind picked up, had her eye on Ernie. It turned out that Ernie had his mind on Yollie, too. He ate a handful of cookies nervously, then asked her for a dance.

"Sure," she said, nearly throwing herself into his arms.

They danced two fast ones before they got a slow one. As they circled under the lanterns, rain began falling, lightly at first. Yollie loved the sound of the raindrops ticking against the leaves. She leaned her head on Ernie's shoulder, though his sweater was scratchy. He felt warm and tender. Yollie could tell that he was in love, and with her, of course. The dance continued successfully, romantically, until it began to pour.

"Everyone, let's go inside—and, boys, carry in the table and the record player," Sister Kelly commanded.

The girls and boys raced into the cafeteria. Inside, the girls, drenched to the bone, hurried to the restrooms to brush their hair and dry themselves. One girl cried because her velvet dress was ruined. Yollie felt sorry for her and helped her dry the dress off with paper towels, but it was no use. The dress was ruined.

Yollie went to a mirror. She looked a little gray now that her mother's makeup had washed away but not as bad as some of the other girls. She combed her damp hair, careful not to pull too hard. She couldn't wait to get back to Ernie.

Yollie bent over to pick up a bobby pin, and shame spread across her face. A black puddle was forming at her feet. Drip, black drip. Drip, black drip. The dye was falling from her dress like black tears. Yollie stood up. Her dress was now the color of ash. She looked around the room. The other girls, unaware of Yollie's problem, were busy grooming themselves. What could she do? Everyone would laugh. They would know she dyed an old dress because she couldn't afford a new one. She hurried from the restroom with her head down, across the cafeteria floor and out the door. She raced through the storm, crying as the rain mixed with her tears and ran into twig-choked gutters.

When she arrived home, her mother was on the couch eating cookies and watching TV.

"How was the dance, *m'ija?* Come watch the show with me. It's really good."

Yollie stomped, head down, to her bedroom. She undressed and threw the dress on the floor.

Her mother came into the room. "What's going on? What's all this racket, baby?"

"The dress. It's cheap! It's no good!" Yollie kicked the dress at her mother and watched it land in her hands. Mrs. Moreno studied it closely but couldn't see what was wrong. "What's the matter? It's just little bit wet."

"The dye came out, that's what."

Mrs. Moreno looked at her hands and saw the grayish dye puddling in the shallow lines of her palms. Poor baby, she thought, her brow darkening as she made a sad face. She wanted to tell her daughter how sorry she was, but she knew it wouldn't help. She walked back to the living room and cried.

The next morning, mother and daughter stayed away from each other. Yollie sat in her room turning the pages of an old *Seventeen,* while her mother watered her plants with a Pepsi bottle.

"Drink, my children," she said loud enough for Yollie to hear. She let the water slurp into pots of coleus and cacti. "Water is all you need. My daughter needs clothes, but I don't have no money."

Yollie tossed her *Seventeen* on her bed. She was embarrassed at last night's tirade. It wasn't her mother's fault that they were poor.

When they sat down together for lunch, they felt awkward about the night before. But Mrs. Moreno had made a fresh stack of tortillas and cooked up a pan of *chile verde,* and that broke the ice. She licked her thumb and smacked her lips.

"You know, honey, we gotta figure a way to make money," Yollie's mother said. "You and me. We don't have to be poor. Remember the Garcias. They made this stupid little tool that fixes cars. They moved away because they're rich. That's why we don't see them no more."

"What can we make?" asked Yollie. She took another tortilla and tore it in half.

"Maybe a screwdriver that works on both ends? Something like that." The mother looked around the room for ideas, but then shrugged. "Let's forget it. It's better to get an education. If you get a good job and have spare time then maybe you can invent something." She rolled her tongue over her lips and cleared her throat. "The county fair hires people. We can get a job there. It will be here next week."

Yollie hated the idea. What would Ernie say if he saw her pitching hay at the cows? How could she go to school smelling like an armful of chickens? "No, they wouldn't hire us," she said.

The phone rang. Yollie lurched from her chair to answer it, thinking it would be Janice wanting to know why she had left. But it was Ernie wondering the same thing. When he found out she wasn't mad at him, he asked if she would like to go to a movie.

"I'll ask," Yollie said, smiling. She covered the phone with her hand and counted to ten. She uncovered the receiver and said, "My mom says it's OK. What are we going to see?"

After Yollie hung up, her mother climbed, grunting,

onto a chair to reach the top shelf in the hall closet. She wondered why she hadn't done it earlier. She reached behind a stack of towels and pushed her chubby hand into the cigar box where she kept her secret stash of money.

"I've been saving a little every month," said Mrs. Moreno. "For you, *m'ija.*" Her mother held up five twenties, a blossom of green that smelled sweeter than flowers on that Saturday. They drove to Macy's and bought a blouse, shoes, and a skirt that would not bleed in rain or any other kind of weather.

THE KARATE KID

It all started when Gilbert's older cousin Raymundo brought over *The Karate Kid* on video. Never before had a message been so clear, never had Gilbert seen his life on TV. As he sat in the dark with a box of Cracker Jacks in his lap, he knew that *he,* Gilbert Sanchez, a fifth-grader at John Burroughs Elementary, was the Karate Kid. Like the kid on the screen, he was pushed around by bullies. He too was a polite kid who did his homework and kept to himself. And, like the kid in the movie, Gilbert wanted to be strong enough to handle anyone who tried to mess with him.

Inspired, Gilbert and Raymundo kicked and chopped imaginary opponents into submission as they walked to the 7-Eleven for a Slurpee.

"The *ninjas* are after us," Gilbert whispered in an alley.

"So what? They can't mess with us. We're cousins. If they mess with you, they mess with me. If they mess with me, they mess with you."

"That's right. We're bad." Gilbert chopped a *ninja* in the neck. "Take that. And that! And give some to your brother."

They climbed on the hood of a wrecked car and stood storklike on one leg, just like in the movie. But instead of crashing sea for a backdrop, there was a dilapidated barrio of ramshackle houses and dusty cars.

Gilbert's courage carried over to the next day. At school, Pete the Heat cut in front of Gilbert while he was in line for lunch. Gilbert looked at him and said, "Hey, the line starts back there."

Pete the Heat, a not-so-bright fourth-grader, was a tough playground fighter who could thump with the big kids.

"What did you say?" asked the Heat. His fists were doubled up and trembling like small animals. He stuck his face into Gilbert's face.

"I said I'm not letting you cut in front of me. Get in back!"

"No, you watch it!"

"I'm not telling you again!" Gilbert doubled his fists and leaned his body into the Heat. He was surprised by his own aggressiveness.

"I'll meet you on the playground," the Heat said, jabbing a finger into Gilbert's chest.

"Any place, any time," Gilbert, to his great surprise,

shouted at the Heat, who cut in closer to the front of the line. Raymundo came up to Gilbert.

"Why did you do that? You know he's a dirty fighter."

" 'Cause," Gilbert said with a faraway look on his face. He was busy picturing himself getting beat up by the Heat.

"You're going to get it," Raymundo warned. "Why did you talk so big, *menso?*"

"Don't worry about it," Gilbert said as he left the line in a daze. He wasn't hungry anymore; he was gorged on fear. Would it hurt much to get smacked in the face lots of times? he wondered. Would he have enough blood left in his body to walk to the principal's office?

Raymundo sat down next to him. He was older than Gilbert and could beat up the Heat, but he knew he shouldn't get involved. It was Gilbert's fight.

"Remember," Raymundo advised, "Chop and kick. Look tough, too."

They met on the playground. Kids closed in to see the fight. Out of the corner of his eye, Gilbert saw Patricia, the girl he liked to think was his girlfriend, walking toward them. Oh no, he thought to himself, she's going to see me get beat up. He wished now that he had let the Heat cut in line.

The Heat said, "What about it, creep! You still think you're bad?"

"Yeah," Gilbert growled. He tried to take Raymundo's advice and sound tough, but his mind had melted into a puddle of misfiring cells. But he wasn't so far gone that he couldn't remember to stand like a stork and flap his arms.

"Just 'cause you seen that *Karate Kid* you think you're

bad, huh? You ain't *bad*," the Heat taunted. Some of the older kids encouraged the Heat to get on with it.

Again Gilbert tried to sound tough. "Come and get me. If you think you're—"

Gilbert never finished his sentence. The Heat caught him with a roundhouse punch to the jaw, sending Gilbert to the ground. The Heat jumped on Gilbert and smacked him a few more times before Raymundo pulled him off.

"That's enough, Heat. Leave him alone."

Gilbert didn't bother to move. A few kids taunted him, called him "sissy," "pushover," and "wimp," but Gilbert stayed on the ground with his eyes closed, waiting for all of them to go away.

Finally, he opened an eye and, seeing that everyone, including Raymundo, had disappeared, rose up on one elbow. How come it didn't work? he asked himself. I stood like a stork, just like in the movie.

Even though it was a school night, Gilbert convinced his mother to let him borrow Raymundo's *Karate Kid* a second time. This time he watched intently, with no Cracker Jacks to distract him. Yes, his school was like the school in the movie, full of bullies. And yes, he had stood like a stork and flapped his arms. But, unlike the kid in the movie, he was smacked to the ground. The missing component struck him like a hammer. He didn't have a teacher, and the kid in the movie did. So that's it, he thought. I need a master to teach me karate.

Gilbert stayed home the next day, feigning sickness, and looked through the *Yellow Pages* for a karate school. It was very confusing. There were so many styles: Shotokan, Taekwon-Do, Kajukenbo, Bok-Fu, Jujitsu, Kung Fu. That one sounded familiar, but it was in north Fresno, far from his home. It would take him forever to bicycle up there.

Finally he decided to call the Shotokan school that was around the corner from his house. He got a recorded message that gave the hours, which were from 3:30 in the afternoon to 7:00 P.M. Gilbert decided to practice standing like a stork until the studio opened. By 3:30 he was exhausted and bored, but he still hopped on his bike and rode over to the studio. The instructor, to Gilbert's surprise, was Mexican, not Japanese like the guy in the movie.

The instructor flipped the sign in the window from Closed to Open and looked at Gilbert. "Hey, kid, what's up?"

He called me "kid," Gilbert thought. I wonder how he knew. Do I look like the boy in the movie?

"You wanna take lessons?"

"Yeah."

"You have to be real serious."

"I will, I promise."

"It's twenty-five a month, and fifteen for the uniform." The instructor let Gilbert in and watched him look around the *dojo,* which was small, dark, and smelly. It held nothing but some mirrors, a punching bag, and a shopping cart full of what looked like boxing gloves.

"And there's an introductory price. Two months for the price of one. Stick around, kid, you look like you'll be good." The instructor bowed at the edge of the wooden karate floor, and walked behind a curtain. After a few minutes he came out wearing his uniform, and all that Gilbert could think was *He's got a black belt.*

Three noisy kids came in clutching grocery bags containing their uniforms. The instructor told them to be quiet, but they ignored him. They took off their shoes but didn't bow the way the instructor bowed when he stepped onto the wooden floor. Gilbert didn't like them because of their rudeness. They were not like the kid in the movie.

Four older kids came in and joined the other kids, who were playing tag. Finally, the instructor clapped his hands together and shouted for them to line up. When one kid whined, "Aw, man," the instructor glared fiercely at him.

"Come on, let's show some respect," he growled.

The kids wiped their sweaty faces on their wrinkled uniforms. As they lined up, one kid pushed another kid, who fell on the ground and pretended to cry. The instructor, pinching his brow into dark lines of disgust, told them to show respect.

The class started with jumping jacks, and even though the instructor told them to stay with the count, the kids jumped as they pleased. He told them to do push-ups, and everyone groaned. Then they sat against the wall to stretch.

Gilbert was in awe. All but two of the seven kids had yellow belts. One had a green belt, and the other wore a white belt with what looked like a piece of black electrical tape on the end.

That night, during dinner, he asked his mother if he could take karate. His mother wiped her mouth and said, "No."

He was ready for this answer, ready for a battle. "How come? It's only twenty-five dollars a month."

"Because you don't need it," his mother said. "You won't learn anything you can use later in life. School is more important."

"Yeah, if you don't get beat up every day."

"What do you mean?" his mother asked.

"I got beat up yesterday by Pete the Heat. That's why I stayed home today."

"Why didn't you say anything?"

"What could you do? You're at work, and I'm at school. You can't hold my hand at recess."

"Don't get smart."

"But it's true. You don't know what it's like."

His mother knew it was true. She stared at her salad and remembered when her parents wouldn't let her take ballet lessons. No matter how much she cried her parents said the same thing: "No, you don't need to." She looked at Gilbert, whose face shone with hope, and asked, "How much are the lessons?"

"Twenty-five dollars. It's cheaper than most places," he said. "And I need a uniform."

She looked at her son's beaming face. "Maybe it'll be good for you," she said.

"I'll train really hard, and then you can call me the Karate Kid." Gilbert ate all his food and washed the dishes without his mother having to ask.

That night he had wild and strange dreams about the whole school watching him pepper the Heat with karate chops and punches. Only when the Heat cried, "No more," did he let up. Then out of kindness and mercy, Gilbert led him to the boys' restroom to wash his bruised face.

Gilbert began his lessons the next day. He was scared of the kids in the yellow belts, though he was as old and tall as most of them.

When Mr. Lopez asked them to bow so they could

begin class, only a few gave courtesy bows. The others nodded their heads or wiped their noses on the backs of their sleeves. Their uniforms were dirty, and their belts were just one wiggle away from coming untied.

"OK, let's do thirty-five jumping jacks," Mr. Lopez commanded.

The kids groaned but started their jumping jacks, out of count with the instructor's. They then did two sets of fifteen push-ups. Again, the kids were out of count and complained that it was too hard.

Gilbert tried to keep up with the instructor but pulled a muscle in his shoulder while doing push-ups. He groaned and said, "Mr. Lopez, my shoulder hurts. Is it supposed to?"

The instructor wrinkled his brow. "You too? The first day of class and you're like the others?"

This made Gilbert try harder. But when it was time to do basic drills, he was at a loss. He looked out of the corner of his eye and saw the other kids moving their arms in patterns. Now and then the instructor would pause long enough to correct Gilbert's mistakes, but most of the time he ignored him and the other boys and gazed out the window at the cars and people passing by.

Next they did kicks—front snap kick, roundhouse kick, side kick—and toward the end of the class the advanced students, those with colored belts, did *katas*. Gilbert sat cross-legged against the wall in awe. But the instructor stood with his hands on his hips, displeased with their technique. He didn't have to say anything, the message was clear.

They ended the class with more jumping jacks and push-ups. The students then "bowed out" and grumbled that it had been the hardest workout in the whole world. Gilbert added a few complaints. His shoulder was sore, and the bottoms of his feet were blistered from the wooden floor. He rode home slowly, with his rolled-up uniform under his arm.

At dinner, his mother, who was secretly pleased that her son was taking karate, asked about his first lesson.

"It was kinda hard," he said, "and I was kinda confused."

Gilbert stood up and did some blocks. He was going to do a front snap kick, but his mother told him to sit down and eat his food before it got cold.

"My feet got some blisters because we practice on a wooden floor." He wanted to show his mother but knew it was impolite to show the bottoms of your feet while someone was eating.

The next week it was pretty much the same thing, jumping jacks and push-ups, stretches that hurt, blocks and kicks, and *katas* at the end of the class.

Gilbert wanted to ask the instructor when he'd get to stand like a stork, the way the Karate Kid did in the movie, but he couldn't catch his eye. Mr. Lopez had a faraway look in his eyes and seemed more interested in watching the people outside than his students.

By the end of the month, Gilbert was bored to tears. Every day it was the same thing. They didn't learn one thing that would protect them from other kids. The instructor himself began to show up late, and even when he was there he didn't bother to correct the students' kicks or blocks. He just walked around the *dojo* with his hands on his hips.

Gilbert wanted to quit, but his mother had paid his

dues for the third and fourth months. When she asked, "How are your lessons? You must be very strong, no?" Gilbert pretended that everything was great and rolled up his shirt sleeve to show off his biceps.

But karate was no fun; it was boring and didn't do him any good. One day at school when Pete the Heat tried to cut in front of Gilbert in the cafeteria line, Gilbert, still convinced in his heart that he was the Karate Kid, shoved him away.

"Didn't I beat you up already?" the Heat taunted.

"You better watch it, Heat. I'm taking karate."

Pete shoved Gilbert and said, "See you on the playground."

Outside, in front of the fifth- and sixth-grade boys, Gilbert assumed a karate stance. The Heat snickered that nothing could save him but the U.S. Army and socked Gilbert in the jaw. The blow sent Gilbert to the ground, where he stayed with his eyes closed until recess was over.

Gilbert was too embarrassed to tell his mother that he wanted to quit karate. She was sure to yell at him. She would say that she wasted over a hundred dollars on karate lessons, that Gilbert was lazy, and, worst of all, that he was scared of the other boys in the class.

Gilbert became as sloppy as the other kids. He went six months, week after week, and advanced to yellow belt, which made him feel proud for a few days. Then it was back to the same routine of sloppiness and the boredom of push-ups and sit-ups, stretching, blocks, kicks, and *katas.* Not once did they spar.

He fantasized about sparring the Heat while Mr. Lopez watched, arms folded over his chest. Gilbert saw himself circle and feint, and he saw the Heat cower and shy away from his blows. But, more often, Gilbert fantasized about quitting. He saw himself fall off his bike and break his leg, or fall off a roof and break his neck. With such injuries no one would taunt him for being a sissy because he couldn't stick it out.

How am I going to tell her? he wondered on the day he decided to quit because it was too boring. Maybe he could tell his mom that the monthly dues were now a hundred a month. Or that he knew enough karate to defend himself. He thought of excuses as he pushed a broom around the karate floor. He looked up and saw his instructor doing a *kata*. The first time he had seen Mr. Lopez perform one he thought he was the strongest man in the entire world. Now he only looked OK. Gilbert figured that anyone who sweated so much couldn't be that good, and the instructor was sweating buckets.

At school the Heat teased Gilbert, saying, "Hey, Karate Kid, let's see what you can do. I bet you can't even whip my sister." It was true. His sister was in Gilbert's grade, and she was as nasty as a cat in a sack.

One day the instructor came in smiling. It was the first time Gilbert had seen his teeth. "I have news for you," he said as the kids lined up. "But not now. Let's practice. Quit fooling around! Line up!" As they did their drill, Gilbert began to smile along with the instructor. I guess this is the day, he thought. Finally we'll get to spar. For months he had obeyed the instructor's yells, and now he and the better-behaved kids were going to get their chance. Gilbert looked at the shopping cart of sparring equipment. He couldn't wait for the instructor to tell them to get the gear.

But the class followed the usual routine. They went up and down the line doing blocks, kicks, and the same. Then the instructor yelled for the kids to fall in line. After hushing them five times, he announced that he was closing the *dojo.* Business had been bad, and he didn't see how he could continue with only twelve students.

"There's nothing I can do," he said, trying to look sad. "Business is business. I'm sorry."

Only one student moaned. The others cheered.

"No respect," muttered the instructor. He yanked on his belt and pointed to the dressing room. "Go! You're terrible kids." The students raced around the *dojo,* laughing and roughhousing, before they changed to their street clothes. They all waved a casual goodbye to the instructor, who was standing at the front window watching the traffic pass.

During dinner that night a smiling and very happy Gilbert told his mom that the studio was closing.

"That's too bad for Mr. Lopez and you kids." His mother was disappointed and, after eating in silence, suggested that Gilbert go to another studio for lessons.

"Oh, no," Gilbert said. "I think I've learned enough to protect myself."

"Well, I don't want to hear about you getting beat up."

"You won't," he promised. And she never did.

Gilbert threw the uniform in the back of his closet and soon forgot his *katas.* When *Karate Kid, Part Two* came to the theater that summer, Raymundo had to see it alone. Gilbert stayed home to read super-hero comic books; they were more real than karate. And they didn't hurt.

LA BAMBA

Manuel was the fourth of seven children and looked like a lot of kids in his neighborhood: black hair, brown face, and skinny legs scuffed from summer play. But summer was giving way to fall: the trees were turning red, the lawns brown, and the pomegranate trees were heavy with fruit. Manuel walked to school in the frosty morning, kicking leaves and thinking of tomorrow's talent show. He was still amazed that he had volunteered. He was going to pretend to sing Ritchie Valens's "La Bamba" before the entire school.

Why did I raise my hand? he asked himself, but in his heart he knew the answer. He yearned for the limelight. He wanted applause as loud as a thunderstorm, and to hear his friends say, "Man, that was bad!" And he wanted to impress the girls, especially Petra Lopez, the second-prettiest girl in his class. The prettiest was already taken by his friend Ernie. Manuel knew he should be reasonable, since he himself was not great-looking, just average.

Manuel kicked through the fresh-fallen leaves. When he got to school he realized he had forgotten his math workbook. If the teacher found out, he would have to stay after school and miss practice for the talent show. But fortunately for him, they did drills that morning.

During lunch Manuel hung around with Benny, who was also in the talent show. Benny was going to play the trumpet in spite of the fat lip he had gotten playing football.

"How do I look?" Manuel asked. He cleared his throat and started moving his lips in pantomime. No words came out, just a hiss that sounded like a snake. Manuel tried to look emotional, flailing his arms on the high notes and opening his eyes and mouth as wide as he could when he came to *"Para bailar la baaaaammmba."*

After Manuel finished, Benny said it looked all right, but suggested Manuel dance while he sang. Manuel thought for a moment and decided it was a good idea.

"Yeah, just think you're like Michael Jackson or someone like that," Benny suggested. "But don't get carried away."

During rehearsal, Mr. Roybal, nervous about his debut as the school's talent coordinator, cursed under his breath when the lever that controlled the speed on the record player jammed.

"Darn," he growled, trying to force the lever. "What's wrong with you?"

"Is it broken?" Manuel asked, bending over for a closer look. It looked all right to him.

Mr. Roybal assured Manuel that he would have a good record player at the talent show, even if it meant bringing his own stereo from home.

Manuel sat in a folding chair, twirling his record on his thumb. He watched a skit about personal hygiene, a mother-and-daughter violin duo, five first-grade girls jumping rope, a karate kid breaking boards, three girls singing "Like a Virgin," and a skit about the pilgrims. If the record player hadn't been broken, he would have gone after the karate kid, an easy act to follow, he told himself.

As he twirled his forty-five record, Manuel thought they had a great talent show. The entire school would be amazed. His mother and father would be proud, and his brothers and sisters would be jealous and pout. It would be a night to remember.

Benny walked onto the stage, raised his trumpet to his mouth, and waited for his cue. Mr. Roybal raised his hand like a symphony conductor and let it fall dramatically. Benny inhaled and blew so loud that Manuel dropped his record, which rolled across the cafeteria floor until it hit a wall. Manuel raced after it, picked it up, and wiped it clean.

"Boy, I'm glad it didn't break," he said with a sigh.

That night Manuel had to do the dishes and a lot of homework, so he could only practice in the shower. In bed he prayed that he wouldn't mess up. He prayed that it wouldn't be like when he was a first-grader. For Science Week he had wired together a C battery and a bulb, and told everyone he had discovered how a flashlight worked. He was so pleased with himself that he practiced for hours pressing the wire to the battery, making the bulb wink a dim, orangish light. He showed it to so many kids in his neighborhood that when it was time to show his class how a flashlight worked, the battery was dead. He pressed the wire to the battery, but the bulb didn't respond. He pressed until his thumb hurt and some kids in the back started snickering.

But Manuel fell asleep confident that nothing would go wrong this time.

The next morning his father and mother beamed at him. They were proud that he was going to be in the talent show.

"I wish you would tell us what you're doing," his mother said. His father, a pharmacist who wore a blue smock with his name on a plastic rectangle, looked up from the newspaper and sided with his wife. "Yes, what are you doing in the talent show?"

"You'll see," Manuel said with his mouth full of Cheerios.

The day whizzed by, and so did his afternoon chores and dinner. Suddenly he was dressed in his best clothes and standing next to Benny backstage, listening to the commotion as the cafeteria filled with school kids and parents. The lights dimmed, and Mr. Roybal, sweaty in a tight suit and a necktie with a large knot, wet his lips and parted the stage curtains.

"Good evening, everyone," the kids behind the curtain heard him say. "Good evening to you," some of the smart-alecky kids said back to him.

"Tonight we bring you the best John Burroughs Elementary has to offer, and I'm sure that you'll be both pleased and amazed that our little school houses so much talent. And now, without further ado, let's get on with the show." He turned and, with a swish of his hand, commanded, "Part the curtain." The curtains parted in jerks. A girl dressed as a toothbrush and a boy dressed as a dirty gray tooth walked onto the stage and sang:

> *Brush, brush, brush*
> *Floss, floss, floss*
> *Gargle the germs away—hey! hey! hey!*

After they finished singing, they turned to Mr. Roybal, who dropped his hand. The toothbrush dashed around the stage after the dirty tooth, which was laughing and having a great time until it slipped and nearly rolled off the stage.

Mr. Roybal jumped out and caught it just in time. "Are you OK?"

The dirty tooth answered, "Ask my dentist," which drew laughter and applause from the audience.

The violin duo played next, and except for one time when the girl got lost, they sounded fine. People applauded, and some even stood up. Then the first-grade girls maneuvered onto the stage while jumping rope. They were all smiles and bouncing ponytails as a hundred cameras flashed at once. Mothers "awhed" and fathers sat up proudly.

The karate kid was next. He did a few kicks, yells, and chops, and finally, when his father held up a board, punched it in two. The audience clapped and looked at each other, wide-eyed with respect. The boy bowed to the audience, and father and son ran off the stage.

Manuel remained behind the stage shivering with fear. He mouthed the words to "La Bamba" and swayed from left to right. Why did he raise his hand and volunteer? Why couldn't he have just sat there like the rest of the kids and not said anything? While the karate kid was on stage, Mr. Roybal, more sweaty than before, took Manuel's forty-five record and placed it on a new record player.

"You ready?" Mr. Roybal asked.

"Yeah . . ."

Mr. Roybal walked back on stage and announced that Manuel Gomez, a fifth-grader in Mrs. Knight's class, was going to pantomime Richie Valens's classic hit "La Bamba."

The cafeteria roared with applause. Manuel was nervous but loved the noisy crowd. He pictured his mother and father applauding loudly and his brothers and sister also clapping, though not as energetically.

Manuel walked on stage and the song started immediately. Glassy-eyed from the shock of being in front of so many people, Manuel moved his lips and swayed in a made-up dance step. He couldn't see his parents, but he could see his brother Mario, who was a year younger, thumb-wrestling with a friend. Mario was wearing Manuel's favorite shirt; he would deal with Mario later. He saw some other kids get up and head for the drinking fountain, and a baby sitting in the middle of an aisle sucking her thumb and watching him intently.

What am I doing here? thought Manuel. This is no fun at all. Everyone was just sitting there. Some people were moving to the beat, but most were just watching him, like they would a monkey at the zoo.

But when Manuel did a fancy dance step, there was a burst of applause and some girls screamed. Manuel tried another dance step. He heard more applause and screams and started getting into the groove as he shivered and snaked like Michael Jackson around the stage. But the record got stuck, and he had to sing

Para bailar la bamba
Para bailar la bamba
Para bailar la bamba
Para bailar la bamba

again and again.

Manuel couldn't believe his bad luck. The audience began to laugh and stand up in their chairs. Manuel remembered how the forty-five record had dropped from his hand and rolled across the cafeteria floor. It probably got scratched, he thought, and now it was stuck, and he was stuck dancing and moving his lips to the same words over and over. He had never been so embarrassed. He would have to ask his parents to move the family out of town.

After Mr. Roybal ripped the needle across the record, Manuel slowed his dance steps to a halt. He didn't know what to do except bow to the audience, which applauded wildly, and scoot off the stage, on the verge of tears. This was worse than the homemade flashlight. At least no one laughed then, they just snickered.

Manuel stood alone, trying hard to hold back the tears as Benny, center stage, played his trumpet. Manuel was jealous because he sounded great, then mad as he recalled that it was Benny's loud trumpet playing that made the forty-five record fly out of his hands. But when the entire cast lined up for a curtain call, Manuel received a burst of applause that was so loud it shook the walls of the cafeteria. Later, as he mingled with the kids and parents, everyone patted him on the shoulder and told him, "Way to go. You were really funny."

Funny? Manuel thought. Did he do something funny?

Funny. Crazy. Hilarious. These were the words people said to him. He was confused, but beyond caring. All he knew was that people were paying attention to him, and his brother and sisters looked at him with a mixture of jealousy and awe. He was going to pull Mario aside and punch him in the arm for wearing his shirt, but he cooled it. He was enjoying the limelight. A teacher brought him cookies and punch, and the popular kids who had never before given him the time of day now clustered around him. Ricardo, the editor of the school bulletin, asked him how he made the needle stick.

"It just happened," Manuel said, crunching on a star-shaped cookie.

At home that night his father, eager to undo the buttons on his shirt and ease into his La-Z-Boy recliner, asked Manuel the same thing, how he managed to make the song stick on the words *"Para bailar la bamba."*

Manuel thought quickly and reached for scientific jargon he had read in magazines. "Easy, Dad. I used laser tracking with high optics and low functional decibels per channel." His proud but confused father told him to be quiet and go to bed.

"Ah, *que niños tan truchas,*" he said as he walked to the kitchen for a glass of milk. "I don't know how you kids nowadays get so smart."

Manuel, feeling happy, went to his bedroom, undressed, and slipped into his pajamas. He looked in the mirror and began to pantomime "La Bamba," but stopped because he was tired of the song. He crawled into bed. The sheets were as cold as the moon that stood over the peach tree in their backyard.

He was relieved that the day was over. Next year, when they asked for volunteers for the talent show, he wouldn't raise his hand. Probably.

THE MARBLE CHAMP

Lupe Medrano, a shy girl who spoke in whispers, was the school's spelling bee champion, winner of the reading contest at the public library three summers in a row, blue ribbon awardee in the science fair, the top student at her piano recital, and the playground grand champion in chess. She was a straight-A student and—not counting kindergarten, when she had been stung by a wasp—never missed one day of elementary school. She had received a small trophy for this honor and had been congratulated by the mayor.

But though Lupe had a razor-sharp mind, she could not make her body, no matter how much she tried, run as fast as the other girls'. She begged her body to move faster, but could never beat anyone in the fifty-yard dash.

The truth was that Lupe was no good in sports. She could not catch a pop-up or figure out in which direction to kick the soccer ball. One time she kicked the ball at her own goal and scored a point for the other team. She was no good at baseball or basketball either, and even had a hard time making a hula hoop stay on her hips.

It wasn't until last year, when she was eleven years old, that she learned how to ride a bike. And even then she had to use training wheels. She could walk in the swimming pool but couldn't swim, and chanced roller skating only when her father held her hand.

"I'll never be good at sports," she fumed one rainy day as she lay on her bed gazing at the shelf her father had made to hold her awards. "I wish I could win something, anything, even marbles."

At the word "marbles," she sat up. "That's it. Maybe I could be good at playing marbles." She hopped out of bed and rummaged through the closet until she found a can full of her brother's marbles. She poured the rich glass treasure on her bed and picked five of the most beautiful marbles.

She smoothed her bedspread and practiced shooting, softly at first so that her aim would be accurate. The marble rolled from her thumb and clicked against the targeted marble. But the target wouldn't budge. She tried again and again. Her aim became accurate, but the power from her thumb made the marble move only an inch or two. Then she realized that the bedspread was slowing the marbles. She also had to admit that her thumb was weaker than the neck of a newborn chick.

She looked out the window. The rain was letting up, but the ground was too muddy to play. She sat cross-legged on the bed, rolling her five marbles between her palms. Yes, she thought, I could play marbles, and marbles is a sport. At that moment she realized that she had only two weeks to practice. The playground championship, the same one her brother had entered the previous year, was coming up. She had a lot to do.

To strengthen her wrists, she decided to do twenty push-ups on her fingertips, five at a time. "One, two, three . . . " she groaned. By the end of the first set she was breathing hard, and her muscles burned from exhaustion. She did one more set and decided that was enough push-ups for the first day.

She squeezed a rubber eraser one hundred times, hoping it would strengthen her thumb. This seemed to work because the next day her thumb was sore. She could hardly hold a marble in her hand, let alone send it flying with power. So Lupe rested that day and listened to her brother, who gave her tips on how to shoot: get low, aim with one eye, and place one knuckle on the ground.

"Think 'eye and thumb'—and let it rip!" he said.

After school the next day she left her homework in her backpack and practiced three hours straight, taking time only to eat a candy bar for energy. With a popsicle stick, she drew an odd-shaped circle and tossed in four marbles. She used her shooter, a milky agate with hypnotic swirls, to blast them. Her thumb *had* become stronger.

After practice, she squeezed the eraser for an hour. She ate dinner with her left hand to spare her shooting hand and said nothing to her parents about her dreams of athletic glory.

Practice, practice, practice. Squeeze, squeeze, squeeze.

Lupe got better and beat her brother and Alfonso, a neighbor kid who was supposed to be a champ.

"Man, she's bad!" Alfonso said. "She can beat the other girls for sure. I think."

The weeks passed quickly. Lupe worked so hard that one day, while she was drying dishes, her mother asked why her thumb was swollen.

"It's muscle," Lupe explained. "I've been practicing for the marbles championship."

"You, honey?" Her mother knew Lupe was no good at sports.

"Yeah. I beat Alfonso, and he's pretty good."

That night, over dinner, Mrs. Medrano said, "Honey, you should see Lupe's thumb."

"Huh?" Mr. Medrano said, wiping his mouth and looking at his daughter.

"Show your father."

"Do I have to?" an embarrassed Lupe asked.

"Go on, show your father."

Reluctantly, Lupe raised her hand and flexed her thumb. You could see the muscle.

The father put down his fork and asked, "What happened?"

"Dad, I've been working out. I've been squeezing an eraser."

"Why?"

"I'm going to enter the marbles championship."

Her father looked at her mother and then back at his daughter. "When is it, honey?"

"This Saturday. Can you come?"

The father had been planning to play racquetball with

a friend Saturday, but he said he would be there. He knew his daughter thought she was no good at sports and he wanted to encourage her. He even rigged some lights in the backyard so she could practice after dark. He squatted with one knee on the ground, entranced by the sight of his daughter easily beating her brother.

The day of the championship began with a cold blustery sky. The sun was a silvery light behind slate clouds.

"I hope it clears up," her father said, rubbing his hands together as he returned from getting the newspaper. They ate breakfast, paced nervously around the house waiting for 10:00 to arrive, and walked the two blocks to the playground (though Mr. Medrano wanted to drive so Lupe wouldn't get tired). She signed up and was assigned her first match on baseball diamond number three.

Lupe, walking between her brother and her father, shook from the cold, not nerves. She took off her mittens, and everyone stared at her thumb. Someone asked, "How can you play with a broken thumb?" Lupe smiled and said nothing.

She beat her first opponent easily, and felt sorry for the girl because she didn't have anyone to cheer for her. Except for her sack of marbles, she was all alone. Lupe invited the girl, whose name was Rachel, to stay with them. She smiled and said, "OK." The four of them walked to a card table in the middle of the outfield, where Lupe was assigned another opponent.

She also beat this girl, a fifth-grader named Yolanda, and asked her to join their group. They proceeded to more matches and more wins, and soon there was a crowd of people following Lupe to the finals to play a girl in a baseball cap. This girl seemed dead serious. She never even looked at Lupe.

"I don't know, Dad, she looks tough."

Rachel hugged Lupe and said, "Go get her."

"You can do it," her father encouraged. "Just think of the marbles, not the girl, and let your thumb do the work."

The other girl broke first and earned one marble. She missed her next shot, and Lupe, one eye closed, her thumb quivering with energy, blasted two marbles out of the circle but missed her next shot. Her opponent earned two more before missing. She stamped her foot and said "Shoot!" The score was three to two in favor of Miss Baseball Cap.

The referee stopped the game. "Back up, please, give them room," he shouted. Onlookers had gathered too tightly around the players.

Lupe then earned three marbles and was set to get her fourth when a gust of wind blew dust in her eyes and she missed badly. Her opponent quickly scored two marbles, tying the game, and moved ahead six to five on a lucky shot. Then she missed, and Lupe, whose eyes felt scratchy when she blinked, relied on instinct and thumb muscle to score the tying point. It was now six to six, with only three marbles left. Lupe blew her nose and studied the angles. She dropped to one knee, steadied her hand, and shot so hard she cracked two marbles from the circle. She was the winner!

"I did it!" Lupe said under her breath. She rose from her knees, which hurt from bending all day, and hugged her father. He hugged her back and smiled.

Everyone clapped, except Miss Baseball Cap, who made a face and stared at the ground. Lupe told her she was a great player, and they shook hands. A newspaper photographer took pictures of the two girls standing shoulder-to-shoulder, with Lupe holding the bigger trophy.

Lupe then played the winner of the boys' division, and after a poor start beat him eleven to four. She blasted the marbles, shattering one into sparkling slivers of glass. Her opponent looked on glumly as Lupe did what she did best—win!

The head referee and the President of the Fresno Marble Association stood with Lupe as she displayed her trophies for the newspaper photographer. Lupe shook hands with everyone, including a dog who had come over to see what the commotion was all about.

That night, the family went out for pizza and set the two trophies on the table for everyone in the restaurant to see. People came up to congratulate Lupe, and she felt a little embarrassed, but her father said the trophies belonged there.

Back home, in the privacy of her bedroom, she placed the trophies on her shelf and was happy. She had always earned honors because of her brains, but winning in sports was a new experience. She thanked her tired thumb. "You did it, thumb. You made me champion." As its reward, Lupe went to the bathroom, filled the bathroom sink with warm water, and let her thumb swim and splash as it pleased. Then she climbed into bed and drifted into a hard-won sleep.

GROWING UP

Now that Maria was a tenth-grader, she felt she was too grown-up to have to go on family vacations. Last year, the family had driven three hundred miles to see their uncle in West Covina. There was nothing to do. The days were hot, with a yellow sky thick with smog they could feel on their fingertips. They played cards and watched game shows on television. After the first four days of doing nothing while the grown-ups sat around talking, the kids finally got to go to Disneyland.

Disneyland stood tall with castles and bright flags. The Matterhorn had wild dips and curves that took your breath away if you closed your eyes and screamed. The Pirates of the Caribbean didn't scare anyone but was fun anyway, and so were the teacups and It's a Small World. The parents spoiled the kids, giving each of them five dollars to spend on trinkets. Maria's younger sister, Irma, bought a Pinocchio coloring book and a candy bracelet. Her brothers, Rudy and John, spent their money on candy that made their teeth blue.

Maria saved her money. She knew everything was overpriced, like the Mickey Mouse balloons you could get for a fraction of the price in Fresno. Of course, the balloon at Hanoian's supermarket didn't have a Mickey Mouse face, but it would bounce and float and eventually pop like any other balloon.

Maria folded her five dollars, tucked it in her red purse, and went on rides until she got sick. After that, she sat on a bench, jealously watching other teenage girls who seemed much better dressed than she was. She felt stricken by poverty. All the screaming kids in nice clothes probably came from homes with swimming pools in their backyards, she thought. Yes, her father was a foreman at a paper mill, and yes, she had a Dough-boy swimming pool in her backyard, but *still,* things were not the same. She had felt poor, and her sundress, which seemed snappy in Fresno, was out of style at Disneyland, where every other kid was wearing Esprit shirts and Guess jeans.

This year Maria's family planned to visit an uncle in San Jose. Her father promised to take them to Great America, but she knew that the grown-ups would sit around talking for days before they remembered the kids and finally got up and did something. They would have to wait until the last day before they could go to Great America. It wasn't worth the boredom.

"Dad, I'm not going this year," Maria said to her father. He sat at the table with the newspaper in front of him.

"What do you mean?" he asked, slowly looking up. He thought a moment and said, "When I was a kid we didn't have the money for vacations. I would have been happy to go with my father."

"I know, I know. You've said that a hundred times," she snapped.

"What did you say?" he asked, pushing his newspaper aside.

Everything went quiet. Maria could hear the hum of the refrigerator and her brothers out in the front yard arguing over a popsicle stick, and her mother in the backyard watering the strip of grass that ran along the patio.

Her father's eyes locked on her with a dark stare. Maria had seen that stare before. She pleaded in a soft daughterly voice, "We never do anything. It's boring. Don't you understand?"

"No, I don't understand. I work all year, and if I want to go on a vacation, then I go. And my family goes too." He took a swallow of ice water, and glared.

"You have it so easy," he continued. "In Chihuahua, my town, we worked hard. You worked, even *los chavalos!* And you showed respect to your parents, something you haven't learned."

Here it comes, Maria thought, stories about his childhood in Mexico. She wanted to stuff her ears with wads of newspaper to keep from hearing him. She could recite his stories word-for-word. She couldn't wait until she was in college and away from them.

"Do you know my father worked in the mines? That he nearly lost his life? And today his lungs are bad." He pounded his chest with hard, dirt-creased knuckles.

Maria pushed back her hair and looked out the window at her brothers running around in the front yard. She couldn't stand it anymore. She got up and walked away, and when he yelled for her to come back, she ignored him. She locked herself in her bedroom and tried to read *Seventeen*, though she could hear hear father complaining to her mother, who had come in when she had heard the yelling.

"Habla con tu mocosa," she heard him say.

She heard the refrigerator door open. He was probably getting a beer, a "cold one," as he would say. She flipped through the pages of her magazine and stopped at a Levi's ad of a girl about her age walking between two happy-looking guys on a beach. She wished she were that girl, that she had another life. She turned the page and thought, I bet you he gets drunk and drives crazy tomorrow.

Maria's mother was putting away a pitcher of Kool-Aid the boys had left out. She looked at her husband, who was fumbling with a wadded-up napkin. His eyes were dark, and his thoughts were on Mexico, where a father was respected and his word, right or wrong, was final. "Rafael, she's growing up; she's a teenager. She talks like that, but she still loves you."

"Sure, and that's how she shows her love, by talking back to her father." He rubbed the back of his neck and turned his head trying to make the stiffness go away. He knew it was true, but he was the man of the house and no daughter of his was going to tell him what to do.

Instead, it was his wife, Eva, who told him what to do.

"Let the girl stay. She's big now. She don't want to go on rides no more. She can stay with her *nina.*"

The father drank his beer and argued, but eventually agreed to let his daughter stay.

The family rose just after six the next day and was ready to go by seven-thirty. Maria stayed in her room. She wanted to apologize to her father but couldn't. She knew that if she said, "Dad, I'm sorry," she would break into tears. Her father wanted to come into her room and say, "We'll do something really special this vacation. Come with us, honey." But it was hard for him to show his emotions around his children, especially when he tried to make up to them.

The mother kissed Maria. "Maria, I want you to clean the house and then walk over to your *nina*'s. I want no monkey business while we're gone, do you hear me?"

"*Sí,* Mama."

"Here's the key. You water the plants inside and turn on the sprinkler every couple of days." She handed Maria the key and hugged her. "You be good. Now, come say goodbye to your father."

Reluctantly, she walked out in her robe to the front yard and, looking down at the ground, said goodbye to her father. The father looked down and said goodbye to the garden hose at his feet.

After they left, Maria lounged in her pajamas listening to the radio and thumbing through magazines. Then she got up, fixed herself a bowl of Cocoa Puffs, and watched "American Bandstand." Her dream was to dance on the show, to look at the camera, smile, and let everyone in Fresno see that she could have a good time, too.

But an ill feeling stirred inside her. She felt awful about

arguing with her father. She felt bad for her mother and two brothers, who would have to spend the next three hours in the car with him. Maybe he would do something crazy, like crash the car on purpose to get back at her, or fall asleep and run the car into an irrigation ditch. And it would be her fault.

She turned the radio to a news station. She listened for half an hour, but most of the news was about warships in the Persian Gulf and a tornado in Texas. There was no mention of her family.

Maria began to calm down because, after all, her father was really nice beneath his gruffness. She dressed slowly, made some swishes with the broom in the kitchen, and let the hose run in a flower bed while she painted her toenails with her mother's polish. Afterward, she called her friend Becky to tell her that her parents had let her stay home, that she was free—for five days at least.

"Great," Becky said. "I wish my mom and dad would go away and let me stay by myself."

"No, I have to stay with my godmother." She made a mental note to give her *nina* a call. "Becky, let's go to the mall and check out the boys."

"All right."

"I'll be over pretty soon."

Maria called her *nina*, who said it was OK for her to go shopping, but to be at her house for dinnertime by six. After hanging up, Maria took off her jeans and T-shirt, and changed into a dress. She went through her mother's closet to borrow a pair of shoes and drenched her wrists in Charlie perfume. She put on coral-pink lipstick and a smudge of blue eyeshadow. She felt beautiful, although a little self-conscious. She took off some of the lipstick and ran water over her wrists to dilute the fragrance.

While she walked the four blocks to Becky's house, she beamed happiness until she passed a man who was on his knees pulling weeds from his flower bed. At his side, a radio was reporting a traffic accident. A big rig had overturned after hitting a car near Salinas, twenty miles from San Jose.

A wave of fear ran through her. Maybe it was *them.* Her smile disappeared, and her shoulders slouched. No, it couldn't be, she thought. Salinas is not that close to San Jose. Then again, maybe her father wanted to travel through Salinas because it was a pretty valley with wide plains and oak trees, and horses and cows that stared as you passed them in your speeding car. But maybe it did happen; maybe they had gotten in an awful wreck.

By the time she got to Becky's house, she was riddled with guilt, since it was she who would have disturbed her father and made him crash.

"Hi," she said to Becky, trying to look cheerful.

"You look terrific, Maria," Becky said. "Mom, look at Maria. Come inside for a bit."

Maria blushed when Becky's mother said she looked gorgeous. She didn't know what to do except stare at the carpet and say, "Thank you, Mrs. Ledesma."

Becky's mother gave them a ride to the mall, but they'd have to take a bus back. The girls first went to Macy's, where they hunted for a sweater, something flashy but not too flashy. Then they left to have a Coke and sit by the fountain under an artificial tree. They watched people walk by, especially the boys, who, they agreed, were dumb but cute nevertheless.

They went to The Gap, where they tried on some skirts, and ventured into The Limited, where they walked up and down the aisles breathing in the rich smells of 100-percent wool and silk. They were about to leave, when Maria heard once again on someone's portable radio that a family had been killed in an auto accident near Salinas. Maria stopped smiling for a moment as she pictured her family's overturned Malibu station wagon.

Becky sensed that something was wrong and asked, "How come you're so quiet?"

Maria forced a smile. "Oh, nothing, I was just thinking."

" 'bout what?"

Maria thought quickly. "Oh, I think I left the water on at home." This could have been true. Maria remembered pulling the hose from the flower bed, but couldn't remember if she had turned the water off.

Afterward they rode the bus home with nothing to show for their three hours of shopping except a small bag of See's candies. But it had been a good day. Two boys had followed them, joking and flirting, and they had flirted back. The girls gave them made-up telephone numbers, then turned away and laughed into their hands.

"They're fools," Becky said, "but cute."

Maria left Becky when they got off the bus, and started off to her *nina*'s house. Then she remembered that the garden hose might still be running at home. She hurried home, clip-clopping clumsily in her mother's shoes.

The garden hose was rolled neatly against the trellis. Maria decided to check the mail and went inside. When she pushed open the door, the living room gave off a quietness she had never heard before. Usually the TV was on, her younger brothers and sister were playing, and her mother could be heard in the kitchen. When the telephone rang, Maria jumped. She kicked off her shoes, ran to the phone, and picked up the receiver only to hear a distant clicking sound.

"Hello, hello?" Maria's heart began to thump. Her mind went wild with possibilities. An accident, she thought, they're in an accident, and it's all my fault. "Who is it? Dad? Mom?"

She hung up and looked around the room. The clock on the television set glowed 5:15. She gathered the mail, changed into jeans, and left for her *nina*'s house with a shopping bag containing her nightie and a toothbrush.

Her *nina* was happy to see her. She took Maria's head in her hands and gave it a loud kiss.

"Dinner is almost ready," she said, gently pulling her inside.

"Oh, good. Becky and I only had popcorn for lunch."

They had a quiet evening together. After dinner, they sat on the porch watching the stars. Maria wanted to ask her *nina* if she had heard from her parents. She wanted to know if the police had called to report that they had gotten into an accident. But she just sat on the porch swing, letting anxiety eat a hole in her soul.

The family was gone for four days. Maria prayed for them, prayed that she would not wake up to a phone call saying that their car had been found in a ditch. She made a list of the ways she could be nicer to them: doing the dishes without being asked, watering the lawn, hugging her father after work, and playing with her youngest brother, even if it bored her to tears.

At night Maria worried herself sick listening to the

radio for news of an accident. She thought of her uncle Shorty and how he fell asleep and crashed his car in the small town of Mendota. He lived confined to a motorized wheelchair and was scarred with burns on the left side of his face.

"Oh, please, don't let anything like that happen to them," she prayed.

In the morning she could barely look at the newspaper. She feared that if she unfolded it, the front page would feature a story about a family from Fresno who had flown off the roller coaster at Great America. Or that a shark had attacked them as they bobbed happily among the white-tipped waves. Something awful is going to happen, she said to herself as she poured Rice Krispies into a bowl.

But nothing happened. Her family returned home, dark from lying on the beach and full of great stories about the Santa Cruz boardwalk and Great America and an Egyptian museum. They had done more this year than in all their previous vacations.

"Oh, we had fun," her mother said, pounding sand from her shoes before entering the house.

Her father gave her a tight hug as her brothers ran by, dark from hours of swimming.

Maria stared at the floor, miffed. How dare they have so much fun? While she worried herself sick about them, they had splashed in the waves, stayed at Great America until nightfall, and eaten at all kinds of restaurants. They even went shopping for fall school clothes.

Feeling resentful as Johnny described a ride that dropped straight down and threw your stomach into your mouth, Maria turned away and went off to her bedroom, where she kicked off her shoes and thumbed through an old *Seventeen.* Her family was alive and as obnoxious as ever. She took back all her promises. From now on she would keep to herself and ignore them. When they asked, "Maria, would you help me," she would pretend not to hear and walk away.

"They're heartless," she muttered. "Here I am worrying about them, and there they are having fun." She thought of the rides they had gone on, the hours of body surfing, the handsome boys she didn't get to see, the restaurants, and the museum. Her eyes filled with tears. For the first time in years, she hugged a doll, the one her grandmother Lupe had stitched together from rags and old clothes.

"Something's wrong with me," she cried softly. She turned on her radio and heard about a single-engined plane that had crashed in Cupertino, a city not far from San Jose. She thought of the plane and the people inside, how the pilot's family would suffer.

She hugged her doll. Something was happening to her, and it might be that she was growing up. When the news ended, and a song started playing, she got up and washed her face without looking in the mirror.

That night the family went out for Chinese food. Although her brothers fooled around, cracked jokes, and spilled a soda, she was happy. She ate a lot, and when her fortune cookie said, "You are mature and sensible," she had to agree. And her father and mother did too. The family drove home singing the words to "La Bamba" along with the car radio.

SPANISH WORDS, PHRASES, AND EXPRESSIONS USED
IN THIS BOOK:

a ver	let's see
abuelitas	grandmothers
chale	no way
chile verde	stew-like dish
chorizo con huevos	spicy sausage with eggs
claro que está bonita	of course it's pretty
comida	meal
dime	tell me
¿dónde andas?	where are you going?

el millonario	the millionaire
empanada	pastry
¿entiendes?	understand?
es demasiado	it's too much
es no problema	it's no problem
es verdad, mi vida	it's true, my dear
ese	man
¿está bonita, no?	it's pretty, isn't it?
estás chiflado	you're crazy
frijoles	beans
guisado de carne	stew
habla con tu mocosa	talk to your snotty girl
hijo	son
"Las Mañanitas"	Mexican birthday song
locos	idiots
los chavalos	the young people
mamacita	little mother
menso, mensa	dummy
mentirosos	liars
m'ija	my daughter
mucho dinero	a lot of money

nada	nothing
nina	godmother
¿no crees?	don't you think?
nopales	pieces of cactus
novios	sweethearts
papas	potatoes
pendejos	fools
puro Mexicano	truly Mexican
que niños tan truchas	what sharp kids
¿qué pasó?	what happened?
quiero hablar contigo	I want to talk with you
saludo de vato	greeting
tienes que estudiar mucho	you have to study a lot
ven	come
viejita	sweet old woman
viejo	old man
¿y por qué cuesta tanto?	how come it costs so much?